**She stroked his face with her hand. "Thank you."**

"What for?" He pressed a kiss to her palm.

"Being there for me. I'm not good at needing anyone, or asking for help," Gina said. "But I wanted to thank you."

"You're welcome. I know you're very strong, and totally self-reliant, but sometimes we all need to lean on someone." A stray tear escaped from her eye, and he wiped it away with his thumb. "I'm here if you need to lean on me. My shoulders can take it."

**Molly Evans** has worked as a nurse from the age of nineteen. She's worked in small rural hospitals, the Indian Health Service, and large research facilities all over the United States. After spending eight years as a Traveling Nurse, she settled down to write in her favourite place—Albuquerque, New Mexico. Within days she met her husband, and has been there ever since. With twenty-two years of nursing experience, she's got a lot of material to use in her writing. She lives in the high desert with her family, three chameleons, two dogs, and has a passion for quilting in whatever spare time she has. Visit Molly at: www.mollyevans.com

**Recent titles by the same author:**

# THE EMERGENCY DOCTOR'S CHOSEN WIFE

BY
MOLLY EVANS

**MILLS & BOON**™
*Pure reading pleasure*™

First published in Great Britain 2008
Harlequin Mills & Boon Limited,
Eton House, 18-24 Paradise Road, Richmond, Surrey TW9 1SR

© Molly Evans 2008

ISBN: 978 0 263 86355 0

Set in Times Roman 10½ on 13¾ pt
03-1008-40812

Printed and bound in Spain
by Litografia Rosés, S.A., Barcelona

# THE EMERGENCY DOCTOR'S CHOSEN WIFE

# CHAPTER ONE

*Hidden Valley, Virginia, U.S.A.*

NURSE GINA RIDDLES stood in the parking lot and looked up at the hospital she had hoped never to enter again. Although necessary, returning here wasn't on her list of fun-filled things to do this summer. Being a travel nurse had been her dream, and she was living it. Over the last few years she'd been there and done it all. Trauma, open-heart surgery, research facilities and cutting-edge university hospitals. She'd worked in many cities and states, traveling as she'd never have been able to if working a permanent job. Travel nursing afforded her the opportunity to visit exotic places and still make a decent living. Coming back here brought her dreams to a screeching halt.

She had hoped she'd be in and out of her home town in a week but unfortunately settling her father's estate hadn't been as simple as she'd hoped. There was so much more involved than packing up his clothing and calling in a maid service.

The honk of a car horn distracted her, and she realized she was in the middle of the parking lot. She moved out of the way and took another look. A sleek, silver, late-model Porsche purred just feet away from her. The driver inched the car forward and zipped down the window.

"Hello. May I help you?"

Gina gulped and felt the thrill all the way to her toenails. Sitting there was the most fabulous-looking man she'd ever seen. Even from behind his designer sunglasses she could see the most piercing blue eyes that cut right through her. The man was gorgeous. Gina's tongue suddenly felt heavy and dry. She doubted she could carry on a conversation and hoped he didn't ask her anything too complicated. Wow. There had been no doctors like this when she had been here six years ago. Certainly none with wavy dark hair with tips kissed by the sun, darkly tanned and fit, like him.

"Are you lost?" he asked, and turned the car into a designated physician spot.

"No. I'm in the right place." His soft, smoky voice almost made her want to follow him around just to hear him speak again. Making a fool of herself the second she arrived at her new job was not the impression she wanted to make. She was a professional. Really.

"Unfolded himself" was the only way to describe how he exited the shiny new car. With a leather brief-case in one hand and a white lab coat in the other, he looked down at her as if waiting for something. With one glance she knew he was someone important. He had that made-from-money look about him. The way he carried himself, the cut of his suit. Everything about him, even the exotic spicy fragrance that drifted on the morning air, whispered *Money*. He removed his sun-glasses, and she knew exactly the kind of man he was.

His family was made from money, old Virginia money, a culture very different from her own. Another reminder of her past that she didn't need today.

"Yes. I'm heading inside, but wanted to take one last breath of fresh air before taking the plunge." She walked alongside him, determined to get through this temporary assignment as well as possible. It was just another job like all the others, right?

"I see. And you are...?" His brows lifted with the question, and he turned those blue eyes on her again.

She held out her hand, and he gave it a brief, firm shake. "Oh, sorry. Gina Riddles, travel nurse."

"Thomas Ferguson, medical director of the ER. Wel-come aboard, Gina. This your first time in Virginia?" he asked, and led the way through the parking area to the staff entrance of the ER.

"No. I grew up here, but haven't been back for a few

years." After this assignment was over she was gone.
She wasn't staying in this place one second longer than
absolutely necessary. Thank God this job was only temporary. She'd see her mother settled and then find
another assignment, on an island somewhere maybe,
where she could relax and catch up on her reading.
Hawaii sounded good.

"Well, welcome back. Let's see about getting you to
the charge nurse."

Gina followed him, trying to live in the moment, not
her past. A past that threatened to take her back to the
place she'd struggled so hard to leave. She tried not to
listen to the erratic beating of her heart. Certainly, it had
nothing to do with this man's unexpected presence and
everything to do with her new job. At least that's what
she tried to convince herself of as she stuck her backpack under the desk.

Thomas frowned as he watched Gina talk with Rhonda,
the charge nurse. A redheaded beauty with flawless skin.
Some hesitation in her blue eyes, though. Hopefully she'd
be more than eye candy. Tall and physically fit, she looked
like a runner and someone who might be able to keep up
with him, biking in the mountains. Certainly he was old
enough and wise enough not to be smitten by a first meeting with a beautiful woman, but there was something
about her. Turning away, he entered his office, puzzled at
the way such a short meeting had intrigued him.

Gina glanced up just as Thomas moved away. Her gaze lingered on his back.

"I see you've met our Dr Thomas," Rhonda said, a knowing smile on her face. "He's something, isn't he?"

"Oh, yeah," Gina said on a breath of a sigh.

Rhonda laughed, and Gina dragged her gaze away. "I'm so sorry. That was really rude, wasn't it?"

"No. Totally understandable. He's very easy on the eye."

"No kidding," Gina said, and snorted at that major understatement. "Now, where were we?"

Hours later, assigned to bring the next patient through Triage, she entered the waiting room. An elderly man rose on trembling knees and clasped a walking cane. Gina strode over to him and offered her arm. "I'm Gina, and I'll be your nurse for a while today." The man took her arm and leaned heavily on it. Unprepared for the movement, Gina compensated and clasped her arm around his thin waist to help support him through the waiting room. "Do you need a wheelchair? I can go get one if it would be easier for you."

"No. I've had too much sitting down as it is," he said. "I can walk that far," he went on, and after a slight hesitation he placed one arm over her shoulders for extra support.

After settling him in a cubicle, Gina started the obligatory history for any patient who entered. "What brings you in today?"

The man cleared his throat and looked away, clearly uncomfortable with whatever he was about to say. "I need a man doctor. Do you have one of them here?"

"A man doctor, hmm? I think we have one around, but I should tell him a little bit about what's going on." She tried to be as gentle as possible with her questions, but did need to get information out of him before dragging a doctor in to see him. "Is it a personal issue?"

"Very. Hasn't been a woman other than my wife seen my privates since I *was* a private. World War Two, you know."

"Gotcha. Is it OK if I check your blood pressure and pulse first so I can tell the doctor I did my job?" Gina asked, and pulled out a BP cuff.

"Sure," he said, and held out his arm, but remained standing beside the gurney.

"You're running a fever. Did you know that?" A temperature was a warning sign of something wrong. The flush to his cheeks didn't look good, and his pulse was irregular. Another sign of trouble. This man definitely needed some help right away. Something in her, some finely tuned nursing instinct, told her there was more to his story.

"Yes, ma'am. Been feeling poorly for some time now." He shook his head in disgust. "Just thought it would go away eventually, but it hasn't."

"*What* did you think would go away?" she asked, and busied herself with her paperwork, hoping that by keeping her eyes averted he would tell her something that he couldn't say while facing her.

"I've got swelling where there shouldn't be any. My thigh and…groin are swollen something awful," he said, shifting his weight again.

Gina removed his shirt and put a patient gown on him, but he kept his pants on. "Can you sit on the gurney, or is it too painful?" Hopefully he could at least lie down and relieve some of the pressure on the groin area. "If you can't sit, I can help you to lie down, which probably will be more comfortable for you."

"I'll try," he said. After removing his trousers while keeping his modesty, Gina assisted him into a reclining position.

Mr Jones was sweating and breathing hard after getting onto the gurney. As a precaution she gave him oxygen. "Sometimes oxygen can help with the pain," she said, and connected the cardiac monitor and automatic blood-pressure cuff as well. One glance at the heart monitor, and she was certain that he was as stable as she could make him for the moment.

"I'll take anything at this point," he said, breathed

deeply and then closed his eyes. The wrinkle between his brows deepened.

"Let me see who I can find for you." Hurrying toward the nurses' station, she almost collided with Dr Ferguson in the hallway. "Doctor? I've got a situation I could use your help with."

"Sure. What's the trouble?" Thomas asked, putting aside the chart he was reading and focusing on Gina.

"I've got a patient who's requesting a male physician. He's apparently very private and wouldn't allow me to examine him properly, but he says his groin is swollen, red and painful. He's also feverish, tachycardic, and in extreme pain. He can't sit very well." Gina hesitated as she watched him digest that information. "I think there's something seriously wrong with him."

"Anything else?" His blue eyes searched hers, his expression unreadable.

Gina swallowed, uncomfortable with his piercing regard. "At this point, no. That's all I've got." She knew she should have had more information to give him, but right now the patient needed the doctor's input.

"Lead the way. Any family with him?"

"No, but he is married." Gina led Thomas to the patient. They entered the cubicle. "Mr Jones? This is Dr Ferguson. He's going to do a more thorough exam." Gina backed out of the way and pulled the curtain around them. "I'll wait outside to give you a bit more privacy. Call me if you need something." Gina tugged the curtain closed.

"So, what seems to be the trouble, Mr Jones? The nurse seemed to think it was of a...delicate nature." Thomas observed the man's flushed cheeks and glanced at the monitor, confirming Gina's assessment of stability.

"It is," Mr Jones said. "I have a...um...condition. It's too painful. I held out as long as I could, but I just don't know what to do about it anymore."

"Oh, I see. Well, how about I take a look?"

Thomas gloved up, preparing to examine the patient. When he eased the gown away, he cringed and tried to keep all expression from his face. *Good God*. He took a deep breath as he assessed the man's affected areas. The groin and upper thigh were red, the skin inflamed and hard as a rock. The left testicle was the size of a grapefruit. "What happened here?"

"I fell and a few days later this is what showed up." Mr Jones shook his head in disgust, but even that small movement seemed to give him pain.

There had to be more to the story than that. "You fell?" That wasn't what his gut was telling him had happened to Mr Jones. Thomas's suspicions were more along the lines of malignancy. The man might have a trauma as well, but that wasn't the only thing wrong with him. Thomas sighed, knowing this wasn't going to be an easy case. But then, easy cases rarely interested him. He liked the intricacies of complicated cases. He knew he should go into hematology or infectious diseases, but his heart was in emergency medicine and the excitement it brought.

"Tripped over the damned cat. Guess I need to get my eyeglass prescription changed, too. Didn't even see her." He winced as Thomas continued the exam.

This was no injury from a fall. Instinct and years of experience told Thomas it was much more than that. The lymph nodes in the left groin and tissue in the upper thigh were swollen, firm, red and painful to the touch. With a sigh, he stood upright. "I'd like to run some tests to figure out what's going on and see if we can't make you more comfortable with a little medication." This wasn't going to be a simple fix or an easy diagnosis. He was certain of it.

Thomas stepped outside the curtain, but he didn't have to look far for Gina.

"So, did you figure out what's going on with him?" she asked, and walked along beside him to the nurses' station.

"Unfortunately, I left my X-ray glasses at home today." He picked up the chart and started writing. "Give him some morphine." Thomas shuddered, sympathetic to Mr Jones's plight. "Then complete lab work-up, X-rays, CT scan, urine culture and blood cultures. We'll also probably have to set up a referral to the hematology-oncology team as well. Have the secretary find

out if they can see him today. This looks pretty urgent."
Thomas scribbled quickly in the chart as he rattled the
orders off to Gina.

"You think he's got cancer, don't you?" she asked,
her eyes wide.

"I think he has *advanced* cancer, and doesn't have a
clue. Tripped over his cat and believes that brought on
this condition," Thomas said, and shook his head.

"Denial is a very powerful coping mechanism," Gina
said, thinking about her own situation with her parents.
"It gets people through a lot of tough situations they
couldn't deal with otherwise."

Thomas didn't respond for a moment, but studied her
wide, expressive eyes clouded with concern for her
patient. The woman was gorgeous. Tall, slender, with
curly red hair pulled back into a clip that somehow
managed to almost contain the mass. Yeah, he'd seen
that before. Not going near that again, no matter how
attractive the package. Once was enough for him. Keeping things professional was his best strategy with the
budding attraction he was starting to feel for Gina. "Are
you *asking* me not to be judgmental?"

"Yes. For just a moment." She bit her lip, hoping she
wasn't leaping off a cliff here.

"Well, you're right," he said, and scribbled some
more on the chart, then handed it to her. "But I still think
he has cancer."

"Thank you, Doctor." She nodded, sending the mass of curling ringlets bobbing.

"Thomas, please."

She gave a quick smile. "Thomas, then." She took the chart from him. "I'll get started on these right away."

Travel nurses. He just didn't get that. Uprooting their lives every three months to go somewhere else and do it all over again. Having come from a family firmly entrenched in Virginia, wanderlust wasn't in his genes. Travelers fulfilled staffing needs, and they certainly had one now. Returning to his charting, he forced himself not to watch Gina walk away, though looking at the back of her was just as attractive as looking at the front. With a sigh of disgust at the surge of hormones racing through his system, he reached for the phone and jerked it off the hook. Now was not the time for him to be falling for a coworker, especially one he'd just met.

Gina approached Mr Jones's cubicle. "Knock, knock. Can I come in?" She peeked through the curtain.

"Yes, ma'am," Mr Jones responded. He lay with his eyes closed, his fingers laced and resting on his abdomen.

"The doctor's ordered some bloodwork and other tests," she said, and took his arm to look for a vein. "As soon as I get an IV started, I'll give you some pain medicine, too. You look like you could use a touch of it right now." In minutes she had the IV fluids going and injected the pain medicine. "Here comes the morphine.

Just breathe slowly and let it go to work." Easing a patient's pain was the most important thing to her as a nurse. Sometimes the pain was physical, sometimes it was emotional. But she did whatever she could to help those in need. That's why she'd become a nurse. She focused on helping others and found a place where she fit in.

Within minutes Mr Jones started to relax and his heart rate decreased by twenty points. "That's better, isn't it?" Gina asked, and patted his arm in a soothing manner. "Now that you're a little more comfortable, I'm going to get you to Radiology for those other tests. Why don't you tell me a little about yourself while I take you over there?"

Several hours later, after all the tests were over, Gina brought Mr Jones back to the cubicle and searched for Thomas. She knocked on his office door. "Dr Ferguson? Um, Thomas? Mr Jones's tests are complete and ready for you to review."

Thomas set down the chart he had been reading. "I'm sure they're not good, but I'll be happy to look at them." He stood with a sigh, disturbed by the task ahead, knowing already what the results would be. Gina hesitated by the door, looking up at him, chewing on her lower lip as worry crept into her eyes. He wanted to put her at ease. He knew he could be demanding sometimes, but he just wanted what was in the patient's best interests. Not that she knew that, being so new to working here. "Something else on your mind?" he asked, and approached her, wanting to see if his reaction to her was any different than it had been this morning.

"I know it's not my place to tell you how to do your job, but…" Some doctors didn't appreciate interference, especially from someone they didn't know. But she wouldn't be acting in her patient's best interests if she didn't say something.

"But what?" Thomas raised a brow and nodded, realizing he was standing very close to her. He took a step back, adding just a little distance between them. "If you have something to say, say it. I appreciate the honesty." Especially after the games his ex had played. Honesty was a refreshing change.

"You have doom and gloom written all over you even before you go in there. He deserves your best face, even if it's not how you feel." Gina tensed, watching Thomas, waiting for him to tear into her. A moment passed, and he said nothing. Surprised that he didn't, Gina waited for him to answer.

"I'm not going to give him false hope if that's what you're asking," Thomas said, and met her gaze squarely. "That's not appropriate."

"If there's any hope at all, it's not false," she said, as they moved away from his office toward the cubicle. "Sometimes people need to have something to believe in, even if they know it's only temporary." Thomas walked along with her, contemplating her words.

"You sound pretty certain of that," he said, and stopped outside the cubicle.

"Unfortunately, I am. Comes from personal experience." Without elaborating further, she pushed aside the curtain. "We're back, Mr Jones."

"What's the word, Doctor?" he asked.

"Mr Jones, I believe it would be prudent to have you stay in the hospital for a day or two to undergo further evaluation." He leaned against the counter in the room and gave a mental sigh. "After the exam and looking at your preliminary test results, I'm thinking that you have cancer in your groin. It wasn't the fall that caused your injuries, but it certainly may have aggravated them."

"Cancer, eh?" Mr Jones said, and blinked several times as he digested the information. "That's a tough one." He rubbed his jaw with his work-callused hand.

"It certainly is. So if there are any treatment options, the oncologist will be able to give you a better prognosis than I can right now." Thomas hated bearing bad news, but it was part of the job. And Gina was right. If there was any hope at all, it wasn't false. He'd do well to remember that.

"OK. If you say so." Mr Jones closed his eyes. "I don't know what I'm going to tell Elizabeth. She's always leaned on me." The long sigh he emitted said it all.

"I'll call Admitting, then," Gina said quietly.

"Go ahead." Thomas watched as she carried out his

orders. Calm, efficient, firm in her beliefs, and not afraid to express her opinion. Interesting combination.

"Got a room on the fourth floor." As Gina leaned over the counter to write, Thomas hesitated. There was something about her that made him want to stop and look. She was certainly attractive and obviously dedicated to her job, but that wasn't enough for him to really notice her. Was it the fiery red hair that was now half out of its clip, or the impish grin that had flitted over her face momentarily? Or was it the glimpse of unmasked vulnerability he had seen in her sparkling blue eyes when they had discussed Mr Jones's case? Maybe that was why she was a traveler, running away from something painful in her life. She'd alluded to it just moments ago. In any case, it wasn't any of his business, and he left the cubicle.

Gina finished writing up her chart and approached Mr Jones. "Hey, handsome. After I take you upstairs, I'll call your wife. She's probably worried about you by now." She knew he was probably trying to protect his wife, but now was not the time to keep this kind of information a secret. Sharing often brought people closer. Except in the case of her parents. But that was a whole different problem. "I'll just grab the paperwork on the way," she said, and stopped with him at the desk. "Are you through with that, Doctor?" she asked. "I'm about to take Mr Jones upstairs."

"Thomas, remember?"

"Sorry." She wrinkled her nose at the slip. "I'm not used to calling doctors by their first names. I'll try," she said, and colored lightly under his amused regard. She schooled herself not to react to that intense stare of his. She'd learned the lesson the hard way years ago that a nice pair of eyes didn't mean anything, and she wasn't about to step over the line again. Once was enough.

"Here you go." He handed her the bundle of mismatched paperwork that served as a chart. "I've added a few new orders for tomorrow."

"Thanks. I'll make sure to pass it along." Gina nodded and gave a quick glance back at Thomas, wondering what he was doing in this town. She knew about his family, and they were the kind that didn't just attend universities, they built them. No great university or research hospitals in Hidden Valley. Just a little town with a whole lot of nobodys in it. She gave a mental shrug. His life was none of her business. Getting curious about him would only bring trouble she didn't need. The phone rang, pulling her away from her thoughts. Thomas picked up the phone, and Gina moved off with the gurney toward the back hallway and the staff elevators.

After taking Mr Jones to his room, getting him settled in, giving the report to the floor nurse and finally returning to the ER, Gina was wiped out. The energy she had spent on her first day on the job had drained her physically and emotionally. Just stepping into this hospital again had made her sweat. She'd done her student nurse training here and had bolted for Richmond, sixty miles away, the day after graduation. From there, she'd taken off and had never looked back. Until now. Until her father's unexpected death had made it apparent that she'd had to come home. But being here was turning into a rope around her neck that was getting tighter and tighter.

Having been away from home for so long, she hadn't realized that things had gotten as bad as they had until it had been too late. Now she was stuck in a quagmire of lifelong guilt, unexpected financial responsibility, and emotional upheaval. She didn't want any of it, but there was no one else, unless she wanted to hand her mother over to the state of Virginia to manage, and that wasn't going to happen. She'd just have to put her feelings aside and deal with it.

Leather briefcase in hand, lab coat tossed carelessly over his shoulder, Thomas approached the nurses' station as he headed toward the door. "I thought you'd left already."

"Don't worry. I'm not going into overtime on my first day. I wanted to see Mr Jones settled upstairs and helped him call his wife." Collecting her backpack, she slung it on and walked with Thomas to the entrance.

"That was kind of you, and I wasn't concerned that you were going over your time."

"Thanks. He doesn't have anybody to be with him right now, so I stayed a few extra minutes. His wife doesn't see well enough at night to drive over here, so I talked to her for a few minutes on the phone." Gina sighed, attempting to shake off the emotions of the day, and tried not see how they mirrored her own life. "I'm beat."

"I'm sure it's been a long first day for you." Thomas held the door open for her.

"Yes, thanks." She started across the parking lot. Humidity in the spring was always oppressive, and it pressed down on her now. "I'll see you tomorrow."

"You're walking?" he asked, his brows raised in surprise.

"Yes. Good exercise." She started to wave, then hesitated as the frown on his face deepened. "What?"

"Gina, really, you shouldn't walk alone at night. That can be dangerous around here."

"It's just a few blocks, Doc. I'll be fine." She lowered her hand and watched as he approached her. Even in the dark, his presence was almost overwhelming. The light from nearby streetlights created shadows on his face that hadn't been there moments ago. The deep-set eyes were hidden and revealed nothing of his mood, and her heart beat a little quicker.

"Nonsense. Come on. I'll give you a ride home." He

opened the door to his car and stowed his belongings in the back.

"Really, it's just a few…" Her throat went dry at the thought of sitting in that little car with such a big man, even if it was just a two-minute drive.

"Then, if it's close by, it won't take any time to deliver you home safely," he said. "I insist."

By his tone and stance, Gina knew there was no sense in arguing with the man, and she was too tired to put up a fight. "Oh, OK. But I really would have been fine. I've walked this town since I was a kid, even at night."

"Things have changed since you lived here. Even in the year since I've been here." Thomas walked around his car. "We've had drugs and gangs infiltrate the schools. Kids are getting into that stuff younger and younger. Not long ago one of our physicians was going to the parking garage and was attacked with a tire iron."

"Oh, my God. Is he or she OK?" Gina asked. "I had no idea stuff like that had been going on." Things like that hadn't happened when she'd been growing up. She'd obviously been way out of touch, more than she'd realized.

"It's a him, and he's OK. He's back at work now, but he was beaten pretty severely." Thomas opened the door for her.

Gina hesitated as she looked inside at the lush leather seats compared to her grungy scrubs.

"What's wrong? Not afraid to ride with me, are you?" A smile twitched at the corners of his mouth.

"No, it's not that," she said, and gave him a sidelong smile.

"What, then?"

"I'm afraid riding in this car will ruin me for all other cars."

Thomas laughed. "What do you drive?"

"I'm afraid to tell you." She tossed her backpack on the floor.

"Gina, I'm not that judgmental."

"OK. It's a Ford. A really old one, but it gets me where I need to go."

"Well, get in and enjoy the ride, even if it's a short one." He chuckled again as she slid into the leather seat with an appreciative groan.

"This should be illegal," she said as he closed the door and went around to the other side.

"So, where to?" He looked across the narrow confines of the car and waited. Despite having never been in a car like this, she looked like she fit it perfectly. With her long legs stretched out in front of her and angled toward him, she looked like she could be in a car commercial. If it weren't for the scrubs she wore.

"Oh, sorry. Take a left out of the parking lot," she said, snapping her seat belt into place and settling into the seat. In minutes they arrived at her cottage. "Could you drive around the block a few times?"

"Why? Do you see someone who shouldn't be there?" he asked and looked up the driveway.

"No. I just wanted to enjoy the ride a little longer. Riding in my car just won't be the same."

He pulled over to the curb and laughed out loud. Glancing in the rearview mirror, he zipped back onto the street. "Once more around the block, just for you," he said. How often had any woman he'd known been made happy with a simple car ride? Never, was the simple answer.

Gina let out a giggle of pleasure that sent a shiver of reaction through him. Here, sitting in the car with nothing else between them, it was easy to forget the rest of his life. But a few minutes later he pulled back into her driveway and the momentary spell was broken. "Here you are," he said, and parked the car.

"Thanks, Thomas. I'm sure I would have been fine walking—"

"But it's better to make sure you got here in one piece. It was no trouble." He glanced at her again, and she held his gaze and he felt himself reluctant to end their drive. "So how was your first day?"

Gina nodded and leaned her head back against the

headrest. "Tiring, but good. I just feel so sorry for Mr Jones."

"Yes, me too. But we'll do whatever we can to help him. I'm sure you know that." He hesitated just a moment. "And I do appreciate the correction you gave me. It's easy to forget that a patient's mental processes aren't the same as ours."

"Yes, it is easy to forget. I just hope there's time for him." She gathered her backpack from the floor and held it in her lap. "My father died of cancer recently, and by the time he was diagnosed it was already too late." What had made her offer that information she didn't know, but being in the car was like being in a secluded bubble where nothing else mattered. "Lord, I must be tired to talk about him."

"I'm sorry. I didn't know. Next time a patient like that comes in, ask to switch if you're uncomfortable with the situation." Thomas scanned her face, but didn't see any obvious anxiety.

"It was OK." Totally different types of men. Totally different types of situations. "My father and I were never close."

Thomas watched the play of emotions across her face and wondered if she could really be as open and honest as she appeared to be. That would be such a refreshing change from the women in his social circles.

Leaning over, Gina reached for the seat belt fastener.

Instead of releasing it, her fingers seemed to fumble and her hand started to sweat, slipping on the polished metal. "I can't get it."

"Let me see," Thomas said, and reached for the buckle, brushing her hands with his. His strong fingers closed over hers and tugged. The buckle came free, and Gina pulled back.

The close proximity of his head to hers in the narrow confines of the vehicle gave her another tantalizing whiff of his cologne. The man smelled like a dream, and her heart fluttered wildly, reacting in ways she hadn't reacted to a man in a long time.

"I guess I should go now." She clutched her backpack to her as if it could protect her from the effect he was having on her. "Thanks again."

"Well, good night, then. I'll watch until you're inside."

"Thanks…Thomas." Gina left the car and walked to her front door. She waved as she entered and locked it again behind her. In seconds she heard the car zoom away. She frowned. He wasn't what she had expected. Taking her home had been out of his way, despite what he had said. He hadn't had to do that. But she was glad he had.

# CHAPTER TWO

AFTER rounds the next day, Thomas decided to visit Mr Jones. His room was across from the nurses' station, and Thomas picked up his chart, but kept an eye on the room. He could see Gina chatting with Mr Jones and an elderly woman Thomas assumed to be Mrs Jones.

Looking through the chart, Thomas read the final test results, which clearly indicated the worst possible news for Mr Jones. He thought about Gina's desire for more time for the man and was sorry that there was little of it left for Mr Jones. The oncologist's note indicated severe disease, recommended a few radiation treatments for comfort, but prognosis was poor at this stage. End-stage cancer with metastases in the lymph, lungs and bone. A CAT scan of the brain was negative. At least that was a somewhat positive note.

There were times that Thomas hated being right, and this was one of them. Looking up at Gina as she threw her head back and laughed, he wondered if she knew. Bearing bad news was something he hated, but it was part of the job of being a physician.

Leaving the desk, he approached Mr Jones's room just as Gina turned. The surprise on her face was obvious, but then there was that impish grin again.

"Hi, Doc. Come on in," she said, then turned to Mr Jones. "Dr Ferguson is here to see you, Harold."

"Harold?" Thomas said and stepped into the room, his brows raised at her familiarity with the patient.

"Yep. We're official friends now," Gina said. "And this is Elizabeth, his wife."

"She's just a delight, Doctor. I feel better just talking to her," Mr Jones said and patted Gina's hand.

"I see." He cleared his throat and assessed Harold's face. Indeed, he did look more relaxed than he had on admission. Having his wife support him through such a time would help him so much. "I see the oncologist was here. Did he have a talk with you?"

"Yes. He gave me the news you started to last night. All bad. But at my age I don't think I'm going to be attempting any treatment." Harold shook his head. "I've lived a good life and want to just make the most of the time I have left." He turned to Elizabeth and they shared an intimate look.

Thomas almost felt an intruder as he watched the loving interaction between them. He watched as Gina looked away, too. There was certainly more to her than met the eye. She wasn't just a beautiful redhead pretending to be a nurse. That she cared about people was obvious. But was she overstepping her role as a nurse, not holding her own professional boundaries?

"My affairs are in order. Having survived two wars, I figured I was pushing my luck already. Now I just want to go home with Elizabeth and not be in pain." Harold nodded, reinforcing his own decision.

"That's right," Elizabeth said, and wiped her eyes. "None of us live for ever. I want him home with me as long as possible."

"That sounds like a very good plan," Thomas agreed. "If there is anything we can do to help you, please, let us know."

"Gina said you people could set me up with help at home. Now that my pain is almost gone, I'd like to get out of here as soon as possible." Harold smiled, eager to convince Thomas of his sincerity.

"Home hospice would be a great service. I'm going to drop in and see him now and then," Gina said, and stood. "Well, I'd better get back to work," she said. "Doc's not paying me to sit and talk all day." She gave Harold's hand a squeeze. "See you soon."

Gina and Thomas departed, approaching the elevator in silence. Gina pushed the button and stared at the numbers on the panel. This man made her uncomfortable. Just standing with him, waiting for the ancient elevator, had her stomach churning. Something about him was very attractive to her, but knowing who he was and the type of lifestyle he came from made her squash any attraction that was beginning to form. She reached out to press the button again. "Why is this thing so slow?"

"Why are you in such a hurry?" he asked, more convinced than ever that there was more to Gina's story than she was letting on. Bad marriage? Bad divorce, like him?

The elevator doors opened, and they stepped into it. "Are you OK?" Thomas asked, observing her closely. She wouldn't meet his gaze, and she hugged her arms around her middle.

"I spent quite a bit of time with Mr Jones, and I just need to get back to the ER. I don't want to get off on the wrong foot on my second day here." Gina shoved her hands into her lab coat and fidgeted in the narrow space. He didn't want to make her any more uncomfortable than she already was, but there was definitely something bothering her.

"That's not a problem. It's been quiet this morning." He hesitated, then looked at her. "You seem a little on edge, though. Are you sure you're OK?"

Gina gave him a surprised glance. "What makes you ask that?"

He shrugged. "I read people well."

"And you're reading something into me?" She'd only

been here two days and already she was falling into the same trap she'd fallen into years ago. No way was that happening again.

Before she could respond, the doors to the elevator opened.

"Gina! Thomas!" Rhonda cried, and motioned for them to hurry. "Trauma coming through the door right now."

Thomas and Gina raced behind Rhonda. Rhonda ushered the family members away and left just the medical team to work on the patient, a young male who appeared to be about sixteen years of age.

Gina hooked up the cardiac monitor and oxygen and started an IV in his blood-covered hand. Though he was unresponsive she talked to him anyway, telling him what she was doing.

"Who knows what happened?" Thomas asked.

"The mother is here, but she's pretty upset," the respiratory therapist said.

"Get her in here," Thomas said, and placed his stethoscope over the patient's chest. "We need as much information from her as possible."

Gina picked up the phone and called the nurses' station. "We need the mother—now."

Seconds later Rhonda escorted a woman near hysterics into the trauma room.

"What happened to your son?" Thomas asked, not looking up as he continued to examine his patient.

"I don't know! Someone dumped him in my driveway looking like this, and I brought him straight here." She sobbed into her hands. "Is he awake?"

"Not yet," Rhonda said. "They're going to be working on him for a while yet."

"This looks like a gang beating," Gina said, and shot a glance at the mother. "I've seen this in other cities. From what you said last night," she added to Thomas, "our little town can't avoid it for ever."

"My son is *not* in a gang," the mother protested, glaring at Gina. "We don't have gangs here. Hidden Valley is too small."

"Richmond's not that far away." Gina knew it, she'd seen it, and hoped this mother would face her son's problems quickly. Denial would only get her so far and then she'd have to face it or deal with the consequences down the line.

"No. It can't be," she cried, and shook her head. "He's just a boy."

"I'm sorry this is such a shock for you. But I just cut off his clothing and found this." Gina exposed the markings on his deltoid for her to see herself.

The mother gasped and pointed a trembling finger at the tattoo clearly defined on her son's arm. "I don't know what that is, but it's not a gang."

"Has he been using any drugs that you're aware of?"

Gina spread the boy's fingers apart, examining them for signs of drug use, but found nothing.

"No." She shook her head and looked as if her world was about to fall apart. "I don't know what's going on."

"Right now we need to focus on stabilizing him. We'll work out the details later," Thomas said. "Rhonda, why don't you take her back to the waiting room?"

"I'll come get you when you can see him, I promise," Gina said, trying to offer the woman some support, though thinking of her son this way was obviously painful. "What's his name?"

"Terrence," the mother whispered. After touching his shoulder, she leaned heavily on Rhonda as they left the trauma room.

"Well, Terrence," Thomas said to the unresponsive patient, "you're in a world of trouble." He turned to Gina. "Let's get a CAT scan. I'm concerned that he hasn't roused at all." He checked Terrence's pupils with a penlight, looking for a response.

"He's had quite a wallop on the back of the head. He may be just concussed or he could have a brain injury," Gina said.

"Absolutely," Thomas replied. He liked the way she thought, processing the possibilities quickly. Obviously a nurse of some experience and ability to think through all the possible scenarios. Good qualities to have in an ER nurse in a small town. Someone who had been around and could snap into emergency mode when the need arose, but be content with the smaller issues of every ER, like the flu, cuts and broken arms. Nurses like that were hard to find. Thomas would have to review Gina's temporary contract and see if he could get her to extend her stay. She'd only been there two days, but working with a nurse with her skills would only make his job easier.

Within the hour Gina handed the boy over to the OR team. Brain surgery was indicated for him immediately.

Gina returned to the trauma room to clean it. Traumas always created a lot of trash.

Thomas found her there, banging drawers, clanging things around and making a lot of noise. He stepped into the room. "What are you doing?" he asked, and looked around. The room looked worse than when the patient had been in there.

"Cleaning," she said, and avoided looking at him. "This room is a disaster." She gathered up the dressing materials that had landed on the floor. "You're a very sloppy doctor, by the way." She gave him a sidelong glance.

"What? I'm not." He frowned at her assessment of his character.

"You are," she said with a smile. "I can see you didn't go to college on a basketball scholarship."

"I didn't, but—"

"You threw a lot of things on the floor and now *I* have

to pick them up." She reached for another handful of trash from the floor. "This is so gross. I think you should do it."

He stepped closer, placing himself inches away from her. She was flirting with him! And he liked it. Hiding a grin, he waited for her to turn round. "I tried for the trash can and missed. That's not sloppy. That's just bad aim."

"Like I said, no basketball scholarship for you." She turned and gasped. She hadn't expected him to be so close to her and her heart took off. She tried to back up, but her legs wouldn't move.

"Want some help with this?" he asked.

"You want to help me?" She glanced down at his attire of crisply pressed white shirt that probably cost more than a day's pay and the navy linen slacks that bore a neat pleat. "You don't want to get blood on your shirt. I can handle this, thanks." The way his mouth moved, one corner of it twitching up, made her want to reach out and touch it, to see if it was as warm as it looked. She swallowed. This attraction was getting a little too serious a little too fast.

He took a step back. "I'm not bothered. Why should you be?"

"Seriously, this is my job, and I'd feel guilty if you helped me. You don't want to be responsible for my guilt, do you?" Despite the mental warning to herself, she couldn't help liking his reply.

"Gina, I've done my share of dirty jobs as an intern and resident. A little bit of gauze isn't going to bother me."

"I know. But just the same. I've got it." She looked down at the mess around her. "It's a shame, isn't it?"

Thomas instinctively knew exactly what she meant. "It is. Some kids learn the hard way, and I think he's one of them."

"His mom's in for a whole lot of heartbreak, isn't she?" Gina asked, already knowing the answer.

"She is. But hopefully she won't have to face it alone." He watched her stuff the gauze into the trash can. "Are you OK?"

"Putting a kid back together gets old sometimes, ya know?" A sigh came from her. "It seems like everywhere I go I put the same kids back together for the same things all the time. Just once I'd like to see them do well."

"Yes. I know. Emergency medicine can be a bit overwhelming at times. Nurses burn out in ICU and ER more frequently than any other area." He watched her with those striking blue eyes. "You make sure to take breaks, don't you?"

"Yes. That's why I don't work in the same area all the time, but change back and forth to stay fresh." Returning to her task, she stuffed more trash in the garbage can.

"Relax, will you? Let someone else get the trash. You don't have to do everything."

"It makes life easier on Housekeeping if I can at least help."

"Certainly. But the trash isn't what's bothering you. Everything is just fine. Terrence is off to surgery and there aren't any other emergencies right now, so why don't you take a break?" He tried to coax a smile out of her, put her mind at ease. "I could use a break, too."

"I can't," she said, as she carried on tidying. "When one job's done, there's always another waiting."

"Come on. Trauma can be tough on people. The patient, the family...*and* the staff," Thomas said, and took a step closer to her, invading her space again, putting more pressure on her until she looked up at him.

She frowned and glared at him, but couldn't hold it and cracked a grin, feeling the heat of a blush in her neck. "What? Don't you have a laceration somewhere to suture?"

"Nope, I'm fresh out." The sassy edge to her voice made him smile. She was a refreshing change from people who knew who he was, what his family was, and sought to ingratiate themselves to him. Gina didn't care who he was, and he liked that.

She dropped her shoulders and released a pent-up breath. "OK. Coffee sounds good. But I need to get rid of this stuff first," she said. "I don't want to leave everything for Housekeeping. That's not fair."

Thomas smiled, glad she had accepted his offer. "Five minutes, in the staffroom, or I'll hunt you down."

She grinned. "Good enough."

Thomas hesitated. When she smiled like that she was absolutely stunning. With a quick nod he left her to her task, not wanting to think where this association could head. They were just coworkers sharing a bit of coffee and conversation, right?

Minutes later Gina entered the staff room to the fragrance of an exotic blend of coffee. "Oh, what's that?" she asked, and sniffed appreciatively. "That's not hospital coffee, is it?" The smell was making her mouth water. Thomas smiled, and Gina's knees threatened to go weak. Oh, he was almost making her mouth water, too.

"This is my secret office stash." He shook his head. "Now you know my deep, dark secret."

"There are some perks to being the medical director, I see."

"So, how do you take yours?" Thomas asked.

"Loads of cream and a touch of sweetener, thanks," Gina said, and accepted the mug from him. For a moment or two she forgot who he was, what he was, and it felt just like two people having a coffee together. Like normal people would. Then she remembered. There was nothing normal about a man like Thomas.

"This isn't your first time in this hospital, is it?" Thomas asked.

Surprised, Gina's brows shot up. "What makes you say that?"

"For a traveler, you seem to know your way around

this hospital very well." Thomas gave a smile. "And your résumé shows that you did your nurse's training here. I looked."

"Cheat. I went to the university program here in Hidden Valley. Then I left right after graduation." Couldn't wait to get out, in fact. And had never thought she'd be back. "Seems like a long time ago."

"Ever think of coming back?" Thomas sipped his coffee and contemplated her. "Being a travel nurse must have its appeal, but when you're ready to settle down, had you thought of coming back here? You have family here, I assume."

Gina cleared her throat and toyed with the cup handle. "My mother's here, but I hadn't thought of returning on a permanent basis." She shrugged and chanced a look at him. "Nothing in my life is permanent, which is why I'm a temporary nurse." Making things permanent meant giving up things she wasn't prepared to give up at this point in her life.

"I see."

Changing the topic, Gina needed to direct the focus away from herself. Sharing personal information didn't come easily. "Your turn, Doc. What brings you to Hidden Valley? If you'll forgive the observation, this doesn't seem like your kind of place."

"Me?" Why *had* he come here? He hadn't thought about it for a long time. To get away? To run away? Not so unlike Gina, he thought. "My life…changed abruptly about a year ago, and I needed a quiet place to think." He paused. Was that really it? "Hidden Valley is a good place to do that."

"Not much to do in a town this size except think, is there? After that, then what? On to bigger and better things?" Gina asked.

"Something like that." But had he thought about what would happen after this? He'd assumed that one day he'd leave, but didn't have any immediate plans to return to the bosom of his family. Being away from them was actually a refreshing change from their high hopes and higher expectations.

"I know what you mean. If you stay here too long, you forget what else is out there." There were so many things she wanted to see and do. But underneath it all she knew there was a loneliness that lingered over her life, no matter where she went. Gina glanced away, unable to hold his vibrant gaze. The man saw things too quickly, too clearly, and she would do well to remember that around him. "But this is a nice place for the summer. After that I'll figure out what I want to do. Traveling does take a lot of energy, having to uproot myself every three months and go somewhere new. But for the most part I like it."

"Why don't you think about staying here for a couple of extra months?" Thomas asked. "Our hospital needs good nurses who know the community, and you certainly fit the need. And you could visit with your mother for a while." He paused. "I'm assuming, of course, that you and your mother get along."

Gina hesitated. "I don't even want to think about it right now. For the time being I want try to relax a little, take a few trips to the mountains, and not have to worry about anything more." Wouldn't that be a lovely change? Not worrying? That's all she'd done since she'd been a kid old enough to figure out what had been going on between her parents. At first she'd been afraid they would divorce, then she'd been afraid they'd stay together. The situation had been no-win from the start. Why they'd stayed together for so many years when they obviously hadn't liked each other remained a mystery to her.

"Fair enough," Thomas said, and they chatted about the hospital until they finished their coffee.

Gina looked away from his intense stare, not liking the way he made her feel. Having a squishy, excited feeling in her stomach for the boss was not good. If things had been different, if they'd had more in common than a job, a shared passion for medicine, if not for her past and his status she might have been able to look into his eyes with honest interest. But she couldn't. Staying away from him was probably her best strategy to avoid repeating her mistakes. Mistakes that had almost cost her dearly.

She returned the mug to the sink and looked at a flyer posted on the message board.

"Are you going?" Thomas asked as he joined her.

"What is it?" She hadn't seen anything of interest.

"It's a fund-raiser for the cancer center. The staff go together to have a little off-time fun together, get dressed up, and raise money for a good cause."

"Since I'm not really part of the staff, I'll probably opt out." Gina's heart rate returned to semi-normal, and she returned to her chair.

"This will be my first time to participate as I've only been here a year, but it's my understanding that the event has been going on for a long time. So us newbies should make an effort to go and be part of the team." Thomas watched her. "What do you think?"

"Uh…no. Why don't I work to relieve any staff member that wants to go?" She shrugged, trying hastily to think up an excuse. Events like that gave her hives. "Travelers usually fill staffing shortages. I don't mind staying behind. Someone has to mind the store."

"We try to include the traveler staff just as much as regular staff because you are part of our team. So far we've enough staffing coverage for the night."

"Oh." Gina considered the event. Who knows? It could be fun. "Where is it going to be?"

"The Boar's Head Inn and Resort. Excellent food."

Gina felt herself stiffen, and her heart tried to pound its way out of her chest.

"Oh, no." Absolutely not. That was the one place in

this town she would never go again. "I can't go." Never, ever again. No way would she go there again and relive the scene of her life's ultimate humiliation. Sick, churning nausea filled her gut just at the thought of it.

"Why not?" he asked. "Have you been to the Boar's Head Inn? It's a charming place that dates back to before the Civil War. The university purchased it some time ago and has done a remarkable job of restoring the grounds and turning it into a first-class resort."

Gina's face went from pale to bright red. "It's not something you would understand, Doc." Really, really wouldn't understand, considering he was one of *them*. "You don't know what it's like to come from the wrong side of the tracks and have people look down their noses at you because you don't have the right last name."

"No, I don't know what that's like. But I personally don't care what side of the tracks you come from as long as you are a decent human being." He frowned down at her. "That's more important."

"That's easy for you to say." Inside, Gina shook from the power of the memories that building evoked. She shouldn't be angry at Thomas because he didn't understand. It wasn't his fault. This was her past, her problem, and hers alone to deal with. "Going into that place brings back all sorts of memories I'd rather not discuss." Her humiliation at the hands of a rich society boy was the last thing she wanted to discuss with Thomas.

"Gina, I don't—"

"No, *I'm* sorry, Doc." She looked into his blue eyes, determined to be honest, despite the cost to her pride. "This is my problem, and I shouldn't be so touchy about it." But the fact was, it still hurt. More her poor judgment than anything else.

"No harm done. But you might consider it an opportunity for personal growth." The smile he gave her was full of compassion and some element she couldn't make out, as if he did understand her pain. "I know a little something about that."

Gina stood and looked away from his gaze. "Thanks for the offer, but I really should get back to work now." She'd even clean bedpans to get out of this conversation.

"Gina," Thomas started, his voice soft. "The fundraiser's for a good cause. Who knows? It might actually be fun."

Gina felt a tremor rip through her. "I can't go," she said, her heart pattering fiercely in her chest. Just thinking about it made her shake. "I don't know my left fork from my right spoon."

"Gina, you're talking nonsense. This is an opportunity to have a little fun with your coworkers and the money raised goes to the university cancer center. The tickets are purchased by the department, so there is no cost to you." He paused and looked deeply into her eyes. "We all have issues. Can't you put yours aside for one night?"

"But…" Gina sputtered in protest, her throat going dry at the thought. Could she do it? Could she actually set foot in that building again? How selfish was she being by not being part of the team?

"Why don't I pick you up?" His eyes gleamed with mischief. "You can ride in my car again."

Gina had to chuckle and some of her anxiety faded away. "Now, that's playing dirty."

"A man's gotta do what a man's gotta do," he said, and rapped his knuckles once on the table, decision made. "Besides, what else do you have to do on the weekends in such a small town?" Was hoping that she didn't have a boyfriend going too far?

"Well, usually, I go to the park or take a drive up the Blue Ridge Parkway. The heat's a lot more tolerable up in the mountains." And it had been her solace for so many years, offering her a silent comfort she hadn't known she'd needed at the time. And now, with her father gone, her mother mentally compromised, she was feeling the need to find that peace again.

"Sounds good. My schedule doesn't allow for much free time except on the weekends, and I could use the time away from my desk."

Gina shifted in her seat and then nodded. "The park is a nice Sunday afternoon spot. Exercise helps with the stress of the job. You're welcome to join me." Would having some time together away from the hospital be a good idea? She didn't know, but what was the harm in a couple of coworkers hanging out together? That's all it was, right? There was no need to delve deeply into their pasts, find out what kind of pain they'd each had or investigate that current of electricity that ran through her every time she came near him. Right?

He smiled again. "I'll take you up on that. Sunday at the park. Now, as for the Boar's Head Inn. Get a nice dress and shoes you can dance in. You might be surprised at how much fun you can have at a fund-raiser." Thomas watched her as she digested that information. "They're not *all* stuffy events."

"You don't know what you're getting yourself into, Doc," she said. "I'm a mess."

"Gina, give yourself a little more credit than that. You're a lovely, professional woman. I'm sure you'll be fine." He patted her on the shoulder, but the gesture failed to reassure her. "Let's get back out there, shall we? I hear a laceration calling my name."

With a reluctant nod Gina left the staff lounge and returned to Triage. This was going to be a busy week.

# CHAPTER THREE

THOMAS usually spent most of his weekends catching up on work. With his family at a safe distance in another town several hours away, no girlfriend and no other pressing commitments, he used this time to do as he pleased. Hiking parts of the Appalachian Trail, mountain biking, and a variety of other solitary sports were his favorites. He went at his own pace and didn't have to talk if he didn't feel like it. Today, some sort of restlessness overtook him, and he found himself staring out the window, rather than wanting to get out his bike or put on his hiking boots. Meeting Gina at the park crossed his mind, but then he stopped. Overlooking the obvious, what could be the result of getting involved with her? They were two people who were going to head in opposite directions soon, so the only thing they could have would be temporary at best. But there was something that drew him back to thinking about her.

He sighed and stretched his back. Why get so philosophical on a beautiful Sunday afternoon? Thomas took a look at the stack of charts piled up on his desk. As the medical director, so many areas required his attention. Not that he hadn't been aware of the requirements when he'd taken the job, but sometimes… He sighed. Sometimes he longed for more freedom and the ease of less responsibility. He suddenly understood the appeal of travel nursing, the ultimate freedom that Gina obviously enjoyed with no commitments and no obligations past a thirteen-week contract. Thinking about her and her carefree lifestyle made him want to pull up stakes and just go somewhere, anywhere, for a few months and not look back. Maybe he could do work for something like Doctors Without Borders or another charitable agency, helping people in the world who had nothing.

But life based on whims wasn't his way. No, his was a prominent family filled with physicians and scientists, prep schools and Ivy League colleges. His life had been planned before his birth, and he had been channeled to fit that family mold. Both of his brothers walked the same path and were also successful in their careers.

His time here in Hidden Valley was limited. He knew that. But for a time he'd needed to come here to lick his wounds and recover from the most brutal experience of his life. This little town had helped him through his divorce, and he enjoyed the surrounding mountains, but something was definitely missing. Something he hadn't anticipated wanting again. Something soft and curvy. Something he hadn't thought he'd miss after his experience with his ex-wife, Constance. But then Gina had wandered in front of him in the parking lot and his thoughts hadn't strayed far from her since.

There had been plenty of available women around, but none had captured his attention as fully as…blue eyes and curly red hair that cascaded down a trim back.

Nearby, the sound of a lawnmower distracted him, and his resolve to work evaporated. It was Sunday, for heaven's sake. He should be out playing, exercising, enjoying himself and flirting with a beautiful redhead, not stuck in his office with nothing more exciting to keep him company than a half-dead house plant. Grabbing his keys, he headed for the park, determined not to let his weekend be a total loss.

After a side trip to a coffee shop for something cold and so full of caffeine his hair stood on end, he looked around for Gina. The park wasn't that big. If she were here, he would find her. Within minutes, a herd of giggling children raced by on Rollerblades, being chased by a redhead in full protective gear, her hair flying out behind her in a long braid.

With a grin, Thomas watched Gina, strangely pleased at her off-hours activity. At least she was enjoying her time traveling. Their contracts were short and they played hard on their assignments. And she was getting more out of her time here in her first week than he had in months.

He pushed away from the car and waited by the sidewalk until the group skated back a few minutes later.

"Hi, Doc! You came," Gina said with a smile of welcome. "I'm surprised." She stopped with the skill of an accomplished Rollerblader.

"Really?"

"Yeah. I figured you were too married to your work to take any time off, even on a Sunday." She panted, catching her breath.

He cringed inwardly. He was way too predictable. "Those are quite a set of blades," he said.

Gina looked down at her hot-pink Rollerblades. "Yeah, they're great. I took an assignment in California once. They have great parks there. You learn fast or you leave your skin on the sidewalk."

"I'll pass on that experience," Thomas said, admiring the long, shapely legs exposed above the blades and below her denim shorts. "Should we sit for a while?"

"Sure. I could use a break." She pulled a bottle of water from her pack and drank, needing to drag her eyes away from the way his simple T-shirt clung to his chest and arms. The man had a physique that said he was active, but didn't spend hours in the gym trying to make himself look artificially muscle bound. She liked that about him. She liked a lot of things about him that she really shouldn't.

"Do you do this all the time?" Thomas asked, and watched as the group of kids raced back in the other direction, their energy seemingly endless, even on a hot spring day.

"As often as I can. Exercise really does help me de-stress. I hike or walk or ride my bike sometimes." She eyed him narrowly. "So what have you been up to today? Nose in the latest issue of *JAMA*, catching up on the latest tropical diseases?" She laughed and drank again.

"I'm ashamed to admit I've spent most of this beautiful weekend in my office, reviewing charts." He shook his head in disgust and drank more coffee.

"Oh, yuck," Gina said with a laugh, and patted his back. "You need to relax more, enjoy life while you can."

"I'm a doctor. I don't know how to relax," Thomas said. "Sad, but true."

"Hasn't anyone ever discussed stress-related illnesses with you?" she asked with a serious nurse look on her face. "If you're going to keep up such a stressful pace, you're looking at an MI by the time you're forty-five. You don't want that, do you?"

"No, you're right." He thought about her words. Though delivered in a light tone, there was a lot of truth to her statements, truth he didn't really want to hear. "Somehow I never pictured myself working as much as I do. I used to play a mean game of golf, but I haven't been out for months. I keep thinking I'll take a day off soon, but it never happens. Something always comes up."

"Am I going to have to have my cardiac patient talk with you?" she asked, her head tilted to the side, her eyes serious, that nurse look still on her face.

"What's that?" Amused, he had to hear this.

"That's the little chat I have with patients who come in with chest pain. Usually men, neglecting themselves so they can get ahead in life. But by the time they get wherever they want to be, they are usually suffering from stress-related illnesses and becoming too debilitated to enjoy their lives."

Thomas looked at her, his gaze wary, her words striking a little too close to home. "Uh, no. I don't think you'll have to have that talk with me. At least, not today."

"Good!" Her face brightened. "Today is too nice to have to be too serious." She shifted her position and faced him. "But you know, Doc, if I've learned one thing in my life, it's that you have to keep trying. No matter what. Set your sights on a goal, and don't let anything get in your way. Not money, not another person, not your place in society. Even if it's something as simple as learning to use Rollerblades, like I did." She held up one foot. "Or a weekly golf game. But you do have to have some kind of balance. You'll have to work on that."

"How did you get to be so smart?" he asked, really wanting to know the answer to that question. Usually people had to suffer in order to have such a philosophy about life, and Thomas wondered what had happened to her. She had the eyes of someone who had experienced great sorrow and something in his soul reacted to that, understood it and commiserated with it.

At that Gina looked away. "Oh, I don't know that it's all that *smart*. More like too stubborn to give up."

Thomas thought about that for a second and a small piece of the puzzle that was Gina snapped into place. Even though he didn't know her whole story, there was pain hidden behind her statements.

"So what was it like, growing up here?" he asked, and took a sip from his glass, but his attention was on Gina.

"Oh, it was pretty quiet."

"Somehow, with you around, I doubt that it was quiet."

Gina clutched her hand over her heart as if pained. "If I were easily offended, I might take exception to that comment."

"I doubt that. What was it *really* like?" He paused, watching her. "I can't see you as the cheerleader type, but you weren't number one in your class either, were you?"

All playfulness left her, and her shoulders stiffened. "You see way more than I gave you credit for, Doc."

"Does that bother you?" He turned to face her fully on the bench, suddenly wanting to know the answer to that. "That I see the real you?" Playing games wasn't his style at all, that was his ex-wife's game, not his. If

he wanted something he went after it in a straightfor-
ward way. Like right now. Being away from work and
getting to know Gina a little on a personal level intrigued him. Scared him, too, if the truth be known.
Part of him hesitated, part of him wanted to charge
forward, and he trembled with the two parts warring
within him.

A flush brightened her face, and her eyes searched
his, then broke away quickly. "There's not much to me,
really." She gave a nervous laugh and drank from her
bottle, but he noticed a slight tremor to her hand.

"Gina—"

"How about we talk about something else for a while?"
she asked, and stood, looking intently off into the distance.

"Sure. About what?" About how strange it felt to be
attracted to a woman for the first time in months? About
how getting involved with a coworker was a bad idea?
About how he had to curl his hands into fists to keep
from reaching out to touch her?

Suddenly she pointed in the direction she was looking. "How about that kid over there who just took a
header off the stair railing. Come on, Doc. We're on
duty." Without waiting to see if he followed her, she
raced across the park.

Thomas dashed after her to a young boy who was
writhing on the ground, clutching his chest and screaming in pain.

"What happened?" Thomas asked, and clasped the boy's wrist to check his pulse.

"He fell off the handrail," another boy beside him said.

"What did he hit?" Thomas asked.

"The pavement," the boy said.

"He means *what body part* hit the pavement?" Gina asked and shook her head.

"Oh. His stomach, I think, but I don't know." The kid scratched his head, trying to remember.

"Can you hear me?" Gina asked, and the kid nodded, still gasping for air. "You need to hold still so we can see what's wrong." As gently as possible they tried to straighten him, but he screamed again, unable to accomplish the move, even with assistance.

"I was afraid of that," Thomas said. "He's probably got fractured ribs." That was only the first of several probable injuries he'd sustained.

"Where's a portable X-ray machine when you need one?" Gina mumbled, trying to cover her nervousness.

"What's his name?" Thomas asked.

"Billy," his friend said.

"He needs to breathe better, Doc," Gina said as the boy gasped for breath. "He's looking a little blue around the gills."

Thomas nodded, pulled out his cell phone and dialed 911.

"They'll be here in a few minutes," Gina said, and

stroked the boy's sweaty hair back from his face. "The station's not far from the park. Just hang on, kiddo."

The boy nodded, but his breathing was still erratic and choppy. Tears poured from his eyes, though he had stopped screaming and allowed Gina to hold him against her.

"Listen to me," Gina said in a soft, soothing tone. "Just listen to my voice and close your eyes. Breathe. Just breathe."

After a few tries Billy was finally able to take a slightly deeper breath, and he started to relax a little against her.

"I'd like to look at his chest," Thomas said, watching Gina calm the boy.

"I'm going to pull your shirt up so Dr Thomas can have a peek," Gina said. "You're lucky there was a doctor in the park." So was she. If she'd had to face this on her own, she'd not have been so calm. But being with Thomas certainly made her feel more confident, whether she actually was or not. Something else she'd never have thought when they'd first met. But now? She didn't know. There was so much about him that didn't match with what she thought she knew about him, his family, men like him.

The red mark of the point of impact spanned the entire width of Billy's chest, with scraped skin all around it. Moving on with his assessment, Thomas pressed his hand into the boy's abdomen, and Billy tensed, pulling his legs up. "Ow," he cried, and clutched his hands to his belly, pushing Thomas's hands away. "That hurts."

"What's your mom's phone number?" Gina asked. "We need to call her right now." Her concerned glance met Thomas's and they knew they had a medical emergency on their hands. "Spleen?" she whispered, and Thomas gave a curt nod.

"No. She'll get mad." Billy shook his head. "She said I could go to the park with Eric for the first time by myself."

"We have to call her, Billy," Gina said in a gentle voice, and patted his arm, brushing off little bits of gravel that stuck to his skin. "I'm sorry, but trust me. She's going to want to know what's happened. She can yell at you later, but right now we've got to get you fixed up." The sound of a siren filled the air. "They won't be able to see us over this hill."

"Stay here. I'll go and flag them down." Thomas stood and jogged over the hill. He returned shortly with the ambulance crawling along behind him. As soon as they had parked near Gina and the boys, the crew dragged out their equipment.

"What do we have here?" one of the paramedics asked, then pulled back in surprise. "Hey, Doc, I didn't realize that was you. What are doing here? Moonlighting at the park?"

Thomas snorted. "As a matter of fact, I was taking some time *away* from the ER this afternoon. But I think Billy here's got possible fractured ribs and ruptured spleen. His abdomen's very tender, so we need him looked at ASAP. He was apparently sliding down the railing on his skateboard and crash-landed on his chest and stomach." Thomas filled in all of the available information as the paramedics took over the situation. "Not a very good idea."

Eric shrugged and looked away. "We've seen other kids do it," he said, and his breathing became rapid and shallow as he watched with tear-filled eyes as his friend was being loaded onto the gurney. "Is he gonna be OK?"

"Not if his mother gets hold of him first. We have to take him to the hospital and have a look at him," the paramedic said. "Why don't you come along, and I'll call your moms from there?"

Whining protests from both boys was the only answer. But getting Billy stabilized was of primary importance. Eric picked up their skateboards and climbed into the front of the ambulance. The crew loaded Billy into the back and took him away, siren blaring, to the hospital.

"Should we go to the hospital to follow up?" Gina asked, and watched the vehicle speed away.

"No. If they need us, they'll call." This was his time off and the boy was in good hands. He didn't need to charge to the rescue and step on another doctor's toes. "Stan is on duty today, and he'll take good care of Billy."

"You're right. Sorry. I have a hard time letting go of something once I get involved. Turning over the case to the ER is the right thing to do," she said, and Roller-bladed slowly back to the bench. "I'm not Supernurse. I can't be everything to everyone."

"Do you really want to be?" he asked.

She blew out a long sigh. "No way."

Thomas followed her, also needing to shake off the effects of the unexpected drama. What was this connection he was starting to feel with Gina? Was it only job related or was it the pain he sensed just under the surface? Or could it be something else, such as simple attraction? He didn't know, but he definitely wanted to. He sat beside her on the bench, staring at her until she looked up at him.

"What?"

"Gina Riddles, I'm going to kiss you."

"What?" Her eyes sprang wide at his unexpected words.

Before either of them had time to think, Thomas leaned over and kissed her on the cheek. "You were great with that kid. You really have a gift for calming people in stressful situations."

Gina puffed out a sigh and glanced at the ground, her face coloring slightly. "Oh. I thought…um…I thought you were…you meant…" Her face and neck turned a remarkable shade of red. "God, I'm so embarrassed."

She clasped her hands over her face and groaned. "Where's an earthquake when you need one?"

Thomas laughed. "Sorry. We're not on a fault line." Thomas placed a finger beneath her chin and tilted her face up to look at him. Fear, relief, yet curious desire pulsed in her eyes, mirroring the emotions churning within him. Her breathing was rapid, but he didn't know if that was from the exertion of exercise or from their close proximity. His own pulse raced, and he knew it wasn't from anything else but being near Gina. Leaning closer, he watched her eyes widen and her pupils dilate. But she didn't pull away. How tempting was that? He looked at her mouth. Her full lips were slightly parted.

"You thought I was going to *kiss* you," he whispered. "Like this?" Thomas pressed his mouth against Gina's and felt a tremble roll through her that echoed in him. Then he pulled away seconds later. Giving in to temptation had not been a good idea. It only made him want to explore more. Which was *really* not a good idea.

"Yeah," she said, and drew in a shaky breath. "Something like that." She stood and pretended to brush something off her shorts. "You know, Doc, it's been an interesting afternoon, but I've got to go."

Though her lips tingled from that kiss, she was not going there ever again. She'd had her fling with a rich guy once, and it had ended in disaster. She wasn't about to repeat that. She had never, ever forgotten that painful life lesson and she wasn't going to forget it now, no matter how deep her attraction to Thomas.

There was so much about this man that she didn't know. So much he didn't know about her. And so much standing between them that she'd never be able to overcome. But it didn't matter. He was out of her league, despite being the most attractive man she'd seen in a long time, despite the flutter that rose in her stomach every time she looked at him. Despite the way he looked at her as if she were a real person, not just someone to satisfy an impulsive sexual need.

Thomas took her hand before she could dash off. "Where are you going? There's still plenty of the day left."

"I just need to go." She tried to tug her hand free, but he refused to release her. She didn't want to be rude and yank her hand away, but the warmth of his skin against hers made her react in ways she didn't want to think about. The contact felt almost comforting, almost right. Almost.

"Go where? I just got here." He hoped it wasn't a date she was running off to.

Gina sighed, hesitating. "I'm going to see my mother, OK?" She tugged again, and Thomas stood, but didn't relinquish her hand.

"Your mother?"

"Yes." Gina refused to look at him. Instead, she reached for her helmet and tucked it under her arm.

"You don't look as if you're about to have an enjoyable outing with her," Thomas said.

"As a matter of fact, I'm not. She's not well." Gina shook her head and sniffed, then wiped her nose as her chin trembled. This situation with her mother was so new, so unexpected, that she hadn't quite learned to deal with the drastic change yet.

Thomas watched her. He hadn't expected her to have such an emotional reaction to a simple question. Was the woman seriously ill? Was that the reason Gina was back? She'd mentioned that her father had recently died, but she didn't seem particularly upset by it. This must be different.

"Has she been ill very long?" He didn't want to probe or push her, but he did want to understand what was going on.

"Longer than I was aware of, I'm ashamed to admit." Gina sat down with a plop.

Something wasn't right here. He didn't know what, but Gina was obviously troubled. "Do you want to talk?" Thomas asked.

"No. There's nothing much to talk about." She gave a harsh laugh, and looked at Thomas as tears filled her eyes. "She can't remember…"

Thomas started to get an idea of what was going on with Gina's mother. "She has some memory…problems?"

"No. There's no problem at all. She has absolutely no memory. Advanced Alzheimer's." Gina looked away from him as her chin trembled again. "She doesn't recognize me anymore."

"I'm so sorry, Gina. That's a very difficult thing to deal with." He wanted to reach out, pull her into his arms and give her the comfort she so obviously needed, but hesitated, wondering how she would interpret that. How it could affect their professional relationship if they shared their personal pain. Once broken, that sort of boundary could never be erected again. Confessions couldn't be retracted.

"Yeah." She nodded. "Denial only goes so far, right?"

"Why don't we just sit here awhile?" Thomas said. "Or we could take a drive up the parkway." He tried to catch her eye, but she avoided his gaze and stared at her hands clenched in her lap. "You said you liked the mountains."

"You're awfully nice to offer, but I'm OK." Gina fiddled with the strap of her helmet.

"I doubt that you're OK, but just the same it's a beautiful afternoon. Why don't we enjoy the rest of it together?"

"Because I'm not very good company." Gina broke off and turned away from him, but he knew she still was crying. Though she made no sound, her shoulders trembled and she pressed her hand to her mouth.

"Come here," he whispered, the sound of her tears breaking down the barriers in his own heart. Propriety no longer seemed to matter. With gentle arms he turned her, pulled her close. Barriers be damned. "I know you think you have nothing to hang on to now, but you can hang on to me for a while."

Gina dropped her helmet and reached out for him. Wrapping her arms around his middle, she pressed her face to his neck and let her tears fall. After a few minutes the tears abated and she pulled away. Her tremulous breathing told him that she was far from fine.

"Is there anything I can do?"

"There's nothing," she said, her voice flat, and she wiped the heels of her hands across her eyes. "Believe me, there's nothing. She has Lewybody dementia. She's only fifty-five years old. It's just a matter of time." After a few shaky breaths, she continued, "My father didn't see any need to take her to a doctor when she was starting to have memory trouble. I don't know that there was much that could have been done, but at least she'd have been cared for."

Thomas closed his eyes and the hope that had briefly flared now died. Unfortunately, Gina was right. If her mother was in the advanced stages, there was nothing to be done except comfort care and letting nature take its course. Instead, there might be something that he could do to help Gina get through this time and adjust to her mother's condition. "You're feeling guilty for not being here, aren't you?"

Gina nodded. "I've been off having a good time on my assignments and totally ignoring the situation at home."

"I'm sure that's not true. You're an adult, you're supposed to be off on your own, enjoying your life. Don't feel bad about that." For the moment Thomas just held her and marveled at how well she fit against him. Gina seemed content to sit in the sunshine with him. "How's her communication?"

"Poor, and it got worse once I moved her out of the house. Most of the time she talks in word-salad, but now and then she has a moment of clarity."

"Where is she?" Thomas reached for her hand, trying to soothe her as the story tumbled out.

"She's in a shelter care, because she obviously can't live alone. I can't take care of her by myself even if I did live here. The bad part is that it needs to be paid for. The house is for sale, but I don't expect to get much out of it." Gina pressed a hand against her forehead with a sigh. "It's not ideal, but I didn't have any choice."

"And this has just been dumped on you in the last few weeks, hasn't it?" He shook his head, trying to understand how she must be feeling.

"Yeah. I came home to help settle my father's estate, but there was no way my mother could live on her own. She was very dependent on my father and when he died I think she just fell apart."

"I can imagine," Thomas responded.

"That's why I took the assignment here. I had to be close by to make sure she was settled. I couldn't just leave her there and take off without making sure she was really going to do OK." Gina wiped her eyes again.

"You're doing a very good thing, Gina," Thomas said. "Don't you have any other family that can help out?"

"No. It's just me." Seeming to get hold of her emotions, Gina took a deep breath. Leaning on Thomas was too easy, too comfortable, and something she wouldn't allow herself to indulge in. She had to be strong on her own. "I'm fine now. Thanks for the shoulder, but I think I've humiliated myself enough for one day." Gina looked at her watch. "Damn. Visiting time is just about over now. They are very strict about not interrupting schedules there. The rest of their residents really respond well to consistency, and I'm hoping she will too." Gina's shoulders slumped. "I won't be able to see her today."

"I'm sorry if I caused the delay."

"No. It's not your fault. Things just happened that way today." She gathered her belongings. "But just the same, I'd better get going. I'll go home and call to see how her day went."

Thomas reached for his cell phone and held it out to her. "If you know the number, you can call right now." Was it selfish of him to want to keep her to himself for a while longer? Or was he being noble and self-sacrificing by wanting to be with Gina during a tough time? He mentally snorted. Hardly. Not while there was a stack of charts a mile high at home, waiting for him.

Gina looked up at him, her gaze guarded. She reached for the phone and dialed. After a short conversation, she returned the phone to Thomas. "Nothing new. Ate well. Happy. Totally demented."

"I'm sorry, Gina. But at least she's happy. She could be a lot worse—paranoid, or combative." The defeat in Gina's voice bothered him more than anything. He hoped it was only temporary.

"I know. I know. She could be a lot better, too. If it hadn't been for my father…she might not be so badly off." Gina bent over and unlaced her Rollerblades, popped the latches and removed her feet. "Oh, that feels much better," she said with a groan of relief.

"I know this is going to sound like a shrink, but it sounds like you need to talk to someone. We're here. It's a beautiful day. Neither of us has plans. Why not?" Really. Why not?

"That's not a good idea, but I appreciate it."

"If you're worried anything will get out, don't. I will keep your confidence."

Gina looked at him, assessing the sincerity in his face and voice. Could she trust this man with her secrets? Trust a man just like the one who had betrayed her? She couldn't hold him responsible for someone else's actions, but they were so alike it was frightening. But dammit, he was right. She did need to talk to someone and the opportunity was right here.

Was she going to let the secrets she'd guarded so long ruin the rest of her life? She sighed, knowing she was at a crossroads. The temptation to get up and run pulsed strong in her veins, an instinct honed for many years. But she'd just gotten through telling Thomas that she was no quitter. How could she back down from her own declaration now?

"OK. But I'm not talking to you about anything else unless you take me for coffee. That looked way too good." She flashed a grin, but knew it was just a delaying tactic. "I can be bought, but I'm not cheap."

Thomas laughed. He picked up her blades and led her to his car. "You're on."

As Gina got in she resisted the temptation to stroke the butter-soft leather seat. This vehicle was a luxury she'd never be able to afford, but she would enjoy it on a temporary basis as they drove to the coffee shop.

This was not a conversation she wanted to share with any eavesdroppers, so they got their drinks to go, stayed in the car, and found a shady place along a deserted, tree-lined lane. Gina tipped her head against the back of the seat and looked out the window. "I used to come here when I was a teenager. The trees have grown up quite a bit in the last few years. They're even more beautiful than they were then."

Thomas looked out at the trees in full foliage as they bent over and seemed to create an archway of emerald leaves that led nowhere. In the fall, those same leaves would be gloriously colored. This was a peaceful place, and he hoped the familiarity would help Gina share her story with him.

Thomas turned toward her, the light in his eyes without judgment or expectation. She needed this. But taking the first step was so very difficult. She wasn't used to needing anyone, and she wasn't comfortable with it.

"So, tell me."

No demands, no recrimination, just a simple opening. That she could live with. But what were going to be the repercussions on their work life? Once intimacies of any sort were shared with a coworker, there was no going back. Things always changed. Whether for the better or not she didn't know. Right now she had to take the chance.

"What do you want to know?"

"Whatever you want to tell. I'll just listen." He shrugged. "Sometimes just the telling of a story can take the starch right out of the problem." He knew it wasn't that simple with her situation, but he wanted to make her feel as comfortable as possible.

Gina sighed, and the story poured out of her. Abusive, alcoholic father. Mother too weak and frightened to stand up to him, even for her child. Gina, the only child, who could never be good enough at anything for words of encouragement or approval.

Thomas hated to ask, but he had to. "Did he ever… hurt you? In any way?"

Gina looked at Thomas. His meaning was very clear. "No. He never touched me. Thankfully. The last time I saw him alive was after I graduated from college." She thought back to that day and tears filled her eyes, but she controlled them, as she'd learned to control them most of her life. "I was so proud to have a real diploma in my hand. Even if it was just a two-year degree, it was a place to start. I wanted him to see that finally I'd done something he could be proud of. I was a nurse, I had a profession, a career, not just a job at the grocery store like everyone else I knew. Or already married with children. I was gonna get out of this town and make something of myself." Gina broke off as her voice cracked. Damn. Emotions were something she hated, couldn't control, and despised that failing in herself. She should be stronger but right now she just couldn't.

"What did he say?" Thomas reached for her hand and placed his on top of it.

"He laughed. He actually laughed. He said no matter what I did or where I went, I'd always be the stupid daughter of an unemployed mill worker." She wiped a tear from her cheek, then took a sip of her drink, trying to cover the tremor in her voice. The touch of his hand comforted her.

"How disappointing."

"That's what he called me. His big disappointment in life." Gina nodded, the bubble of heat and remembered pain in her chest throbbing.

"Not you, *him*!" Thomas turned her to face him in the small confines of the vehicle. "None of that is true, Gina. None of it." He searched her eyes, trying to find a way to make her see the truth in his, and the lie in her father's words. Words that had controlled her life for too many years. He could see it, but Gina was the one who had to believe it. "You should be very proud of yourself. Graduating from nursing school is a great accomplishment. I know he was your father, but he was just plain wrong." Her background was vastly different from his. He'd been expected to attend college, medical school, and he'd never doubted the rightness of it. But to be thwarted at every turn was just plain cruel. "I'm very sorry your parents weren't more supportive of you. You've done very well despite the problems."

Tears flooded Gina's eyes, and her chin trembled, her pain palpable. "I don't want it to be true, but I'm so afraid that he's right."

"No, he's not." Thomas drew her to him. This time he couldn't stop, and didn't want to. He kissed her. He needed to kiss her, and she needed to be kissed. By him, right now.

The feel of her, the taste of her, the silky glide of her tongue against his urged him on, and he breathed in the scent of her. He took the kiss deeper, wanting to sense everything about her. Her trembling hands reached out to cup his face, and he held on to her, wanting more than he should right now.

Pulling back, he held her close. "Gina, I'm sorry if I've overstepped my bounds, but I've wanted to kiss you since the day you walked into the ER."

With a quick laugh, she pulled back a little, wanting to see his eyes. The passion in them stunned her, and her heart responded erratically. His touch thrilled her, and his kiss stirred her more deeply than she'd ever known a kiss could. But what she saw in Thomas's eyes frightened her. She'd never live up to his expectations, she knew that. With his background, how could she?

Thomas brushed her face with his hand, pushing away the tears and leaving only the unmasked desire exposed. "You don't know how refreshing you are to me. Why don't you think about staying on for a while?" There. He'd said what he'd been thinking for days now. Why not? Her mother was here. It made sense, didn't it? "You could be closer to your mother, have a little more stability in your life." He paused with a dangerous thought poised on his tongue. "And…we could get to know each other."

Stunned, Gina sat back in the seat. The sound of his

smoky voice almost lulled her into dropping her emotional barriers and reaching out to him as she hadn't
reached out to a man in years. "When I was young I got
to know a guy like you." Memories of the past intruded
bring reality back to this almost magical moment.

Thomas held her gaze. "What happened?"

"I loved him with all of my heart." She looked down
at her clenched fists. "He humiliated me in the worst
possible way, used me. Coming back here has brought
back memories I'd rather forget." She shuddered. "I
haven't dated very much since then."

Thomas didn't say anything for a moment, then he
reached out and cupped her face in his hands, raising her
gaze to his. "I'm not that guy."

She smiled and said softly, "I know. But you understand why I'm fairly hesitant about staying here any
longer than I have to. Too much of my past is wrapped
up here, and I don't want to fall back into being that person anymore."

"I do understand. But you've got to put your past to
bed sometime. You might try it while you're here." He
released her and started the car. "For now, I'd better get
you home before I change my mind."

"About what?" Gina asked with a frown.

Thomas laughed and took her hand, kissed the
knuckles and then put the car in gear. "About whether
I want to take you home."

"Oh, God. I'm so sorry! I can walk from the park. It's not a problem. I didn't mean to inconvenience you." She hurriedly gathered her things. God, she was *so stupid*.

"Gina, wait," Thomas said, his voice serious, and he placed a hand on her arm to stop her hurried movements. "I'll take you home if you want. I'd just rather not end our day yet."

# CHAPTER FOUR

"Oh." She gave a quick laugh and tried to make that flutter in her stomach to go away, but it wasn't going anywhere. "Well, dinner and a bottle of wine wouldn't be out of the question. We've both got to eat, right?" Gina said, her voice soft. She kept her gaze to her lap, watching her clenched fists. Had she just said that out loud?

"Well, I've no dinner plans." When he smiled across at her, she tried to ignore that squiggle in the pit of her stomach.

He carried on, "We'll stop by the store to get something for dinner, then go to my place, relax and cook a meal together."

"Sounds good to me. I'm suddenly feeling hungrier than I have all day." With Thomas, the day seemed to have brightened, and she was reluctant to let go of the feelings he brought out in her. Her burden did seem to have lightened a bit in the sharing of it with him. Spending time in her lonely cottage had little appeal.

As they entered the market a few minutes later, Gina was telling Thomas about an assignment she'd been on when a squeal from the bakery counter startled her into shocked silence.

"Gina! Gina Riddles! Is that you?" a female voice called from halfway across the store.

Gina stopped and turned, a stunned smile plastered on her face, and waited for the woman to come round the display of summer produce.

"Brace yourself," she whispered to Thomas out of the side of her mouth.

"What—"

"Mary Lou? Is that really you?" Gina asked, suddenly acquiring a thick Virginia accent.

Thomas's jaw dropped as a woman charged across the store toward them.

"Gina! It *is* you," Mary Lou squealed, and dragged Gina into an exuberant hug that made her teeth ache. "I heard you was back in town. I was so sorry to hear about your momma, and your daddy, too, God rest his poor soul." Mary Lou clucked her tongue and pulled back to look at Gina, but didn't relinquish her grip on Gina's arm.

"Yep. It's me. Back in town. Here I am." Gina knew she was babbling, but any information this woman gained was going to be all over town in a matter of minutes.

There were grapevines and then there were small-town grapevines that put the speed of the Internet to shame.

"Now, who's your fella here? Why, isn't this Doc McPherson from the hospital?" Mary Lou turned to Thomas, an expectant look on her face.

"It's Ferguson," Gina corrected with a tight smile, not liking the way Mary Lou looked Thomas up and down, her brown eyes lingering in places they shouldn't. "Mary Lou Arnold, this is Dr Thomas Ferguson, Medical Director of the hospital ER. Thomas, Mary Lou and I went to high school together." A thousand years ago, it seemed. Not nearly long enough ago, she thought as years of memories came tumbling back down on her head like a fallen tower of blocks.

"Pleased to meet you. So, you and Gina are together? She's a nurse now, you know," Mary Lou said, her eyes shining with admiration as she elbowed Gina in the ribs.

"No, we're not together," Gina said with a frown, her head beginning to ache. "Yes, we work together at the hospital. I'm on a *temporary* assignment there, Mary Lou. I'll only be in town for a few months, then I go to another assignment somewhere else." She had to stop any rumors before they took on a life of their own. She'd lived here. She knew how it worked.

"Uh-huh," Mary Lou said, her eyes gleaming. "You'd better hold on to this one, honey. He's a doctor, and a looker, too. Those are hard to come by in one package."

"Yes, well, Mary Lou," Gina interrupted with a sudden desire to steer the topic away from her and Thomas and any liaison she might cook up. "How old are your babies now?"

"Oh, why, Gary is twelve, Eddie is ten, and the little one, Jessie, is seven already." Mary Lou ticked them off on her fingers.

"Three children in five years?" Thomas asked, his brows raised. "Impressive."

Mary Lou patted her generous hips with a look of pride on her face. "These were made for makin' babies. But thank God Vernon got himself snipped or we'd have a pile more."

"So, Mary Lou, what kind of specials do you have today?" Gina asked, trying to change the subject away from Mary Lou's hips, babies, and the past. She glanced at Thomas and caught amusement sparkling in his eyes. Damn. At this rate, she'd be talking about her past all night long.

"Steaks. We've got a real nice rib-eye steak, or fresh Atlantic salmon steaks on special. Just come on over here." She took Gina's arm again and led the way. "I'll chase Irving out from behind the counter where he's hiding. He does that, you know." Mary Lou released Gina's arm and charged through the doors to the butcher. "Irving! Come on out here."

"What was that all about?" Thomas asked, obviously trying not to laugh but failing miserably.

"You've gone and done it now, Doc." Gina shook her head, but she bit her lips together to keep a grin from exploding onto her face. Thomas had a way of bringing out inappropriate laughter in her. Warmth bubbled in her chest. She shouldn't feel anything for Thomas except friendship, but every time she looked at him she sank deep into his eyes and didn't want to come out. No man had ever had that kind of appeal before. And she didn't quite know what to make of it. Should she pull away or take one tiny step toward him?

"Me? What did I do?" He pressed his hands to his chest, all innocence.

"You're charming and cute. We've been seen together…in public. That's all it takes to start a rumor around here. By tomorrow I'll be on welfare, having your baby out of wedlock and shaming my family for the next ten generations to come," Gina said, and shook her head.

"Are you kidding? She's going to get all that out of a simple introduction?" Thomas looked at the door through which Mary Lou had disappeared.

"You know people see and think what they want to. Just wait," Gina said, knowing that rumors spread like wildfire during a drought. But at least now Mary Lou's enthusiasm seemed relatively harmless. Gina was older, wiser, and wasn't going to be hurt by the sniping of others ever again. At least, that was what she was telling herself today. Somehow, with Thomas standing beside her, she did feel stronger and able to handle whatever came her way.

Mary Lou dragged Irving out by his arm. "Here he is."

"Now, what can I get you folks?" Irving asked, and tried to extricate his arm from Mary Lou's grip.

"Give me a man-sized steak and something a little more delicate for the lady," Thomas said, and pulled Gina against his side with a big grin.

Gina's mouth dropped, and she elbowed Thomas in the ribs. "Thomas!"

"See? Didn't I tell ya?" Mary Lou said to Irving, and smiled widely.

"So, when's the weddin'?" Irving asked as he wrapped the steaks.

Gina hung her head in defeat and covered her eyes with her hand. Another wildfire was going to rage out of control.

"Don't you worry about nothin', honey. I'll help you plan everything," Mary Lou said, and handed Gina a glossy brochure. "I make the best weddin' cakes in town."

"You're a dead man," Gina said, and watched as Thomas cooked the steaks at his house on an indoor kitchen grill, which pulled the smoke down and out through a hidden ventilation system.

With a laugh, Thomas touched his glass of wine to Gina's. "I couldn't help myself. That was so much fun, seeing the looks on their faces."

"Oh, well, mark my words, by tomorrow the paper will be running our engagement announcement because of that little stunt of yours." She laughed. "Your family will think you've gone off at the deep end." But for some reason it didn't bother her that much. She'd be leaving town in a few months, then the gossips would have something and someone else to talk about. Maybe she'd grown, maybe it was the wine, maybe it was Thomas's supportive presence, but she no longer cared. At least for now.

"My family will know better if anything should come of it. If you're bothered by it, though, I can go and talk to Mary Lou and set her straight." Thomas tossed two potatoes into the microwave and turned it on.

Gina held up one hand, her eyes wide. "No! Don't you dare. That will only fuel the fire that we've had a lovers' spat or something." She waved her hand, dismissing the idea, and sipped her wine, trying to cover the tremor in her hand.

"I'm a little confused, though," Thomas said as he layered a salad and mixed it up. "She's got a twelve-year-old, but you've only been out of school ten years. How'd that happen?"

"The usual way, Doc. Are you sure you went to med

school?" Gina twitched her brows at him. "I said we went to school together. Only one of us graduated. She had her first baby at sixteen and dropped out. I'm a rebel because I chose to go to nursing school and not look for a husband."

Thomas burst out laughing and dropped a cherry tomato into the salad bowl. "You've got to be kidding!"

"Unfortunately, no." A wave of sadness washed over her, and she drank from her glass again, needing a bit of fortitude. "This is why I've avoided coming back here for so long. Rumors and gossip can ruin a life, and I no longer want to be attached to any of it."

Thomas stepped around the counter and closer to her, his proximity forcing her to look up at him. "If something is true, then it's not a rumor, right?"

"I...I don't know quite what you mean." She swallowed, her throat suddenly tight, and her stomach clenched. Thomas was too close, too right, too male. Too sexy. He'd said he was attracted to her. That in itself was intoxicating. His presence so close beside her stirred her senses and almost overwhelmed her. She licked her lips and tried to breathe normally, tried not to let her emotions run away with her, but the closer he got the harder that became. And now she was less sure she wanted to resist it. After all, how long had it been since she'd let a man touch her? Was she going to let one bad experience ruin her life?

After the stress of the last few weeks, she could use a little comfort.

"I mean, if we're dating, then it's not really a rumor, is it?" He curved his hand around her ear, pushing her hair back from her face.

The touch was so gentle, so intimate that a thread of need pulled tight in her belly. A need she hadn't acknowledged for a very long time threatened to unravel, and she wanted to pull on it to see how long it lasted. "Thomas," she whispered as the feeling in her stomach blossomed into outright lust. Lifting her face, she waited for him to make the next move. "What am I doing here?"

"What do you mean?"

"I mean, what are we doing, you and me? Together?"

"We're having a meal, getting to know each other." He shrugged. "Pretty simple."

"I haven't been on a date in two years," she said.

"Neither have I."

"So…why now? Why me?" She dropped her gaze. "I'm sure there are lots of women who'd be more appropriate for you."

"Appropriate?" He laughed. "What's that supposed to mean?"

"I'm just not the kind of woman you usually date, am I?"

"No, you're not."

See? She'd known it. Deep down, she'd known and

had deluded herself that he'd really have been interested in her. Just a rehash of her past.

"Do you have any idea what a breath of fresh air you are?" he whispered, inches from her face, his gaze on her mouth.

Startled, she looked up at him. He was so close she could see the flecks in his eyes, smell his aftershave, and feel the electricity humming off of him. "Now I really don't know what you mean."

"What I mean is, you don't play games. Your honesty is very attractive. You don't care who I am, you still tell me I'm a lousy shot—which I am, by the way." He smiled and the corners of his eyes crinkled up. "You've not let who I am turn you into something you're not, and that's very attractive."

She grinned, his words making her feel better, but a squiggle of caution lingered.

"You're not sitting in my kitchen because of some political or social advantage. You're a darling, Gina. That's all." Without another word, Thomas closed the distance between them and took her mouth with his. Breathing in his fragrance, his maleness, and the scent of *burning steak*, Gina pulled back with a gasp. "Steak!"

"Damn," Thomas said, and turned off the grill. "It can wait," he said, and dragged her against him. Gina surrendered to his kiss.

The ache inside her burst free and she pressed against

him, needing to feel the length of him against her. She wrapped her arms around his shoulders. Desire flared inside her, and she answered the heated probe of his tongue, wanting more. Needing him against her. Needing to be needed, if only for this moment.

Thomas spread hot kisses across her cheek and down her neck. She dropped her head back, giving him access, reveling in the sensations swirling in her body. Her body reacted instantly, and she wanted him now, more than anything she'd ever wanted. Right or not, she wanted him to want her. Going too fast wasn't her way, but today her way had been derailed. Just once she wanted to live in the moment. Just once.

With a groan, Thomas held her tight, spreading hot, wet kisses over her hair and forehead. His breathing was as erratic as hers, and she felt his heartbeat matching the fluttering pace of hers.

"Gina." He breathed her name in her ear, and she shivered. He picked her up and seated her on the kitchen counter. He stepped between her knees so they were eye to eye.

"But—"

"Shh." His hands gentle, Thomas dragged his fingertips up her arms and goose bumps raced across her flesh. Her nipples hardened and ached for his touch. He bent to her neck and pressed his mouth to her collarbone, slowly tracing it with his tongue, leaving a moist trail behind. He brought his large hands to cup her face. "Look at me, Gina," he said. "I want to see your eyes."

Reluctantly, she brought her gaze to meet his intense stare and gasped at the open, unmasked desire there. The thread inside her that had once been tightly coiled completely unraveled.

"You are beautiful, Gina. Beautiful," he whispered.

Groaning with unleashed desire, she fisted her hands in his hair. She wanted more, wanted all of it. Now. Consequences be damned.

The microwave pinged.

Thomas pulled away with a groan. Bracing his arms on either side of her hips on the counter, he tried to gain control of himself. Gina didn't touch him, afraid that if she did neither one of them would be able to let go.

Gina blew out a breath and dragged her hand through her hair, pulling it back from her face. "Wow."

Thomas laughed and looked up at her. "Wow is right." Finally, he stood upright and stepped a few paces away. He poured a glass of water, took a few gulps and handed it to Gina. She pressed the cool glass to her cheek and then drank, wanting to pour it right over her head.

"Let me see if I can rescue our steaks," Thomas said, and busied himself at the grill.

Gina jumped down from the counter. "I can help with the other stuff," she said, and took the bowl of salad to the table. "This looks really great. Thanks for doing all the work." Nerves made her hands slippery with sweat, and she clutched the bowl, hoping she wouldn't drop it.

Steering the conversation away from the heat that sparked between them seemed to calm them both, though the electricity of attraction only faded into the background. They chatted about work and patients, telling stories to each other about unusual cases they had both encountered. By the end of the evening Gina had completely forgotten to be nervous. Any anxiety about her past or new rumors about to begin were forgotten.

"So, your turn. Tell me about you," she said.

"Me, huh?" He speared a piece of steak but didn't eat. He sighed. "Divorced."

"That was your big derailment last year, wasn't it?" Gina felt sad for him. Only a great love could turn into such a great hurt.

"It was. I came here to try to understand what happened."

"What did happen?" It sounded like he needed to talk, too.

"I wasn't enough." He shrugged.

"Are you kidding?" A man like him with looks, charm, came from a great family, kissed like a fantasy, and smelled like heaven wasn't enough for the woman? "She's nuts."

Thomas leaned back in his chair and roared with laughter.

"Oh, God. I can't believe I said that out loud," Gina said, and buried her face in her hands. "That was so lame."

"Yes, it was. But you're right. Nothing pleased her. She was more interested in what being married to my name meant than being married to me. There was nothing I could do to change that, so I gave her a settlement and walked away. It was best for both of us."

The tiniest bit of pleasure flared in Gina's chest. She was glad the woman was gone from his life. Even if nothing came from her budding relationship with him, he deserved better than that.

He shrugged. "I'm just glad we didn't have children to drag through that mess."

"Do you want them?"

"Sure. Someday." Thomas finished his wine and stared at her.

"What is it?" she asked, resisting the urge to reach up and pat her hair into place.

"Nothing. I just like looking at you," he said.

"Oh." The nervousness that she'd forgotten surged back to her stomach, and a bright flush warmed her cheeks.

"I've made you uncomfortable now. I didn't mean to." He reached over and took her hand in his. "I was just really enjoying the company."

She shrugged. "It's OK." She brought her gaze up and met his. "I like looking at you, too."

He stood and assisted her to her feet. "On that note, I think I'd better get you home."

Gina looked at the clock and was surprised to see it was nearly ten. "I've overstayed my welcome. I'm so sorry, Thomas. Why didn't you say anything?"

"I enjoyed myself, and you have not overstayed your welcome at all. You are welcome here anytime," he said, and grabbed the car keys off the counter. "But the reality is that tomorrow is Monday morning, and we've both got to be at work."

"Though I hate reality, it's where we live, isn't it?" she said. "I don't work until the afternoon, but you have to get up early, don't you?"

"Unfortunately, yes."

As Thomas drove to her cottage a comfortable silence filled the space between them.

"Thank you for an unexpectedly lovely day," she said as he parked the car in the driveway.

"You are quite welcome, Gina," he said, and got out of the car.

"You don't have to walk me up, it's OK," she said as they walked round the car. "I'm used to doing for myself, and it won't be any trouble."

"No trouble at all," he said as he escorted her up the walk to the front door. "I always walk my dates to the door."

"This wasn't really a date," she replied, and fished in her pocket for her keys, her hands trembling.

With his gentle hands on her shoulders he turned her to face him. "If tonight wasn't really a date, then this isn't really a kiss, is it?" Slowly, he bent down to her.

Unable to even think of resisting, Gina lifted her face and parted her lips for his kiss. Something about the softness of his mouth against hers, the way he pressed her against the door and stroked his tongue over hers made her want to abandon all caution and invite him inside. As his mouth explored hers, her pulse sang in her ears. When at last he released her, Gina felt every heartbeat rock through her system.

"What is going on between us, Doc?" she asked. "What is this?" She had to know if he felt the same way she did. Was it real or was she just having a great fantasy?

"I think this is called a serious attraction," he said, and pressed a kiss to her forehead. "I'd like to see you again."

"You'll be seeing me again. We work—"

"I mean like this." He cupped her face and brought her mouth to meet his again. Nodding, Gina closed her eyes and rubbed her face against his neck, savoring the feel, the smell and the taste of him. The anticipation of what it could all mean. "I'd like that."

"I know we'll see each other at work, but I'll pick you up on Saturday evening at six for the fund-raiser."

"You really want me to go with you?" she asked, her

insides twisting at the thought. Another thing she'd forgotten about in Thomas's presence.

Looking into her eyes, he said, "I really want you to go with me. I want to hold you on the dance floor and make every man in the room jealous."

Gina laughed and pressed the back of her hand to her nose to control the snort that threatened to disgrace her. "Oh, I doubt that will happen. But I'll go with you. Just don't say I didn't warn you."

Thomas grinned and kissed her knuckles. "It's a date. See you tomorrow."

Thomas couldn't concentrate on the discharge planning meeting or any of the other meetings he attended. Why did these meetings always have to be scheduled on Mondays? Despite his best efforts, nothing held his attention for more than a few minutes. His mind was on the surprising events of yesterday.

"What do you think, Dr Ferguson?" Marge, the discharge planner, asked him.

Damn. "Could you repeat that, please?" he asked and shuffled the paperwork to at least appear as if he was interested.

"Discharge tomorrow planned for Harold Jones, with a recommendation of hospice care at home. I can send the referral information today and get it set up." Marge looked at him, expecting an intelligent response.

"Good idea. He hasn't changed his mind to bypass any form of treatment, has he?"

"No, no treatment," Marge said. "He's opting for palliative care only."

"Having read the oncologist's note, it seems the best course," Thomas replied, and they moved on to the next patient.

Monday was a non-stop circus of meetings that sucked the life out of him, and Thomas couldn't wait for the end of the day. Shutting himself into his office after lunch, he made an attempt at the charts in front of him. The formerly mundane task now became a source of irritation he didn't want to deal with. By three o'clock he was ready to tear his hair out in anticipation of Gina's arrival on shift. But that time came and went without her.

"Where's Gina?" he asked Rhonda. "Isn't she due on shift?"

"Yes, but she switched with someone else for today." Rhonda showed him the staffing book and the approved swapping of shifts. "Is that a problem? Since it was an equal switch, I didn't see any reason to involve you."

He frowned. Was Gina trying to avoid him after last night? "No problem. Is she OK?"

"Yes, but her mother fell and broke her hip last night. She's upstairs on the ward. Room 332."

Without a word, Thomas strode to the elevator, concerned for Gina and her mother. A serious fall for an Alzheimer's patient could be devastating. He hoped that Gina was OK and wasn't worrying too much.

He left the elevators, took the chart from the rack and approached the room. Gina sat clutching her mother's hand, her head on the edge of the bed. She was asleep. Looking at the circles beneath Gina's eyes, Thomas felt his heart contract. She was exhausted. Thomas stood in the doorway and read the chart.

"So, what do you think, Doc?" Gina's soft, sleepy voice interrupted him as she sat up and scraped the hair back from her face, revealing marks from the bedding imprinted on one cheek.

"Looks like a serious break. The orthopod has been here, seems to think she'll survive the surgery OK. Psych has a different story. So does Anesthesia." Didn't they always? But hospital care was about finding the balance between too much and not enough, what you *could* do and what you *should* do.

"Yes, she's been very agitated. She was just getting used to the routine at the shelter care, now she's in another environment, lots of strangers, and in pain." Gina fingered a well-worn rag doll that lay on the bed beside her. "I brought her doll over. She calls it Dina. It used to be mine." She half-smiled and her watery gaze sought out Thomas's. "I like to pretend it's me. That somehow in her mixed-up mind she remembers me in some way. At least, that's what I tell myself."

Thomas entered the room and stooped beside Gina. "She may. It may be the only way she can communicate now. Sometimes a trauma can cause the communication to decrease or stop altogether. You have to be prepared for that."

Gina placed her hand on Thomas's cheek and nodded. "I know. I know. Doesn't make it any easier, though. Thanks for coming."

"You could have called me. I wouldn't have minded." He took her hand in his and kissed her palm.

"Gina, honey? Is that you?" Martha asked, her eyes bright and, for once, clear, staring straight at Gina.

"Mama!" Gina gasped and her heart pounded. "It's me, Mama. It's me." *Please, oh, please, let her talk to me just this one time. Just once, that's all I want.*

"Where have you been? I've been worried about you," Martha said, and Gina's heart broke all over again. For just one moment she'd thought… "I promise I'll come see you every day, Mama." Tears pricked Gina's eyes. For the last two days it seemed as if all she'd done had been cry. Was it ever going to stop?

"Hello, Martha. My name is Thomas," he said in a soft voice.

"Do *you* know my Gina?" Martha asked, as if Gina weren't sitting beside her, the moment of clarity gone.

"Yes, I know your Gina. She's a wonderful daughter, isn't she?" Thomas asked, trying to wring every ounce of conversation out of this one brief moment.

"Yes. My Gina is a good girl." Martha reached out to him, and Thomas took her hand. "Can you tell her to come and see me? She doesn't see me anymore."

Sobbing, Gina leaned over in the chair and buried her face in her lap.

"I'll do my best, Martha. Do you want me to tell her anything?" He cleared his throat as Gina's muffled tears tore at his heart.

Martha picked up the doll and examined it as if she didn't know what it was. "I love her. She's a good girl. I miss her."

"I'll tell her. Why don't you try to get some rest now?" His throat was tight, and he pulled the blanket up to her chin and tucked her in.

"I don't like it here. Come here, my Dina," Martha said, and hugged the doll to her chest and closed her eyes with the contented sigh of a small child. "I'm going home."

Thomas drew Gina to her feet and escorted her to the back stairs and down to the physicians' parking lot. Sobbing the entire way, Gina didn't ask any questions but let Thomas lead her along. Once they were on the road, Thomas called the hospital. "Rhonda, I'm leaving early today. Something urgent came up. I'll be on my cell if you need me." He flipped the phone shut and drove home.

After tucking Gina into his bed, he lay next to her and held her until she slept.

# CHAPTER FIVE

GINA opened her eyes and came face-to-face with Thomas. His eyes were closed and his long eyelashes almost touched his cheeks. He was beautiful. She started to reach out to him, then paused.

The memory of the past two days came rushing back to her. She sucked in a breath and Thomas opened his eyes, blinked, then focused on her.

"How are you?" he asked.

"I was having the most wonderful dream," she said, still trying to shake herself from it.

"What was it about?"

Though he hadn't moved, she felt his energy, his compassion reach out to her, and something in her heart reacted.

"I was up in the mountains. Alone. I don't know where I was, but it was beautiful and peaceful. I've been up in the mountains many times, but this place was a slice of heaven." Oh, to be able to go back there and recapture the essence of that dream would be wonderful.

"It sounds lovely." His hand cupped her face and his thumb stroked over her lower lip, his gaze dropping to her mouth. "So, how are you really?"

"I've had better times," she said, and stroked his face. "Thank you."

"What for?" He pressed a kiss to her palm.

"Being there for me. I'm not good at needing anyone, or asking for help," Gina said. "But I wanted to thank you."

"You're welcome. I know you're strong and are self-reliant, but sometimes we all need to lean on someone." A stray tear escaped from her eye, and he wiped it away with his thumb. "I'm here if you need to lean on me. My shoulders can take it."

"Thomas…I do need you. I just don't know…how to ask you, what to say, how to feel right now. Everything is happening so fast." God, she didn't want to want him so much, but right now he was the only solid thing in her rapidly changing world.

"No matter what else happens between us, you can trust me," Thomas said, his voice a soft whisper that echoed in her heart.

Gina wished that time would stop right now. That she could live in this moment for ever and never have to worry about anything again. Being this close to a man was very unusual for her. But there was something about Thomas that kept drawing her back to him. Could she trust him, as he'd said? Could she reach out and take what he seemed to offer her?

Falling for him wasn't a good idea. In fact, it was a really *bad* idea. But right now she didn't care. She needed him. She had nothing, and no one else, except what was right in front of her.

"What time is it?" she asked.

"About eight."

"Eight?" She sat bolt upright and flung off the covers. "I can't believe I slept so long. I need to call the hospital and check on my mother."

"I called an hour ago, and she's been sedated again. She'll rest through the night."

"Thank you, Thomas." Gina settled back on the bed and pressed a hand to her forehead as dizziness assailed her. She hadn't eaten all day. But nothing was as important as doing everything she could for her mother, even if all she could do was check on her by phone.

"Why don't I get you something to eat? You must be hungry by now." Thomas sat up and swung his legs over the edge of the bed.

"If you've got peanut butter, just a sandwich will do."

"What bachelor worth his salt doesn't have a jar of peanut butter?" Thomas held out his hand to her and pulled her upright. "Come on."

Gina allowed him to lead her to the kitchen for a glass of milk and a sandwich. She ate in silence.

"By the way, I took you off the schedule for a few days until the situation with your mother is sorted."

"You did what? Thomas, I'm on a contract, and I have to work a certain—" How could he make a decision like that without even asking her? The peanut butter stuck in her throat.

"Wait. Just wait. I called your company, explained that there was a family emergency. They've agreed to add the days onto the end of your contract without any penalty." He gave her a lopsided smile. "No worries, OK."

Sighing, the relief she experienced was enormous. "Thomas, you're getting me more indebted to you all the time. I'll never be able to repay your kindness," Gina said. What would happen when she took another assignment and left Hidden Valley? They were both destined to get hurt if they kept this up. There was no way around it. He was firmly entrenched here, and she was rooted…nowhere. Wouldn't it be nice to come home to this every night? Peanut butter sandwiches when you need them.

"You don't have to. I'm doing this because I want to, not so you owe me something." Thomas searched her eyes for answers to questions he didn't even know how to ask. He reached out and cupped her cheek with his hand. Her skin was so soft that he wanted to touch her more and more. "Did he hurt you that badly?"

She didn't need to ask who the "he" was. Though she tried to pull away, he kept his hand on her face. "I don't want to do this."

"Gina, I don't want to hurt you."

"I don't want to get hurt either. But if we keep this up, one of us is bound to lose."

"It doesn't have to be that way. I want to get to know you, but you have to meet me halfway." Was he falling in love with her? Was it just desire and circumstances between them? Would they have had the same attraction between them if they had met at another time, another place without the drama of the workplace?

"I just don't understand why you want to. Why me? Why not some society woman who knows all the right people, does all the right things, rather than someone like me?" What could he possibly see in her? She was nothing.

"I don't know, Gina. I don't know. All I know is that you're here, exactly where I want you." He took a breath and stepped closer. "There's an old saying that goes something like, 'Never ask why. Just accept the good things in life.' And so I am. Even when they come at me out of nowhere." He stared right at her as he said it.

"I'm not…I don't know how…" She shook her head. The good things in life just didn't happen to people like her. If they did, she'd have had a better life a long time ago, not the one she lived now. "What if…?" The words wouldn't come out.

"Shh." He placed a finger to her lips. "Just accept."

"I'm not used to needing anyone, but I do need you, Thomas." She took a trembling breath, determined to see this through. Somehow she needed to start living again. "I need you, but I'm afraid of reaching out."

"Just like everyone else in this world."

With a nod, Gina admitted to herself that he was right. He'd been there too.

"I've been to this dance a few times myself. It stinks, and I don't want to go there any more than you do. But I'm even more afraid of not living my life."

"But…what if I can't stop being afraid?" That was truly her greatest fear.

"Eventually, you'll have to trust yourself enough to find out." He continued to stare at her, seeming to wait for her, allowing her the space she needed.

Need and desire warred within her, battling with the fear she'd lived with for most of her life. "You're right," she said with tears in her eyes. "What is life without experiences? I don't want to wake up when I'm eighty and look back on life and I wish I had." She held out her hand to him, and he took it, entwining his long fingers with hers.

"None of us knows the future. It's the here and now that counts."

With a tug, he pulled her closer, and she went to him, her fears curiously subdued with those simple words. "Thomas…" Shedding everything except for her need for him, Gina reached out and held him.

"Will you stay with me?" he asked, sliding one hand into her hair and cupping the back of her head as he waited for her answer. Desire seemed to flow from him in his posture, in his eyes, in the set of his jaw. He hungered for her. She wanted him.

"Yes." The word was a sigh in her mouth, and Thomas moved. His mouth was made of magic as he kissed her. The silky glide of his moist lips coursing over hers made her wonder why she had ever questioned this. This need for him was real. Holding him in her arms was real. She'd never been passionate, but he brought it out in her.

"I want your skin against mine," he whispered against her mouth. Long fingers tunneled under her shirt and stroked up her back, pulling goose bumps along the way.

She shivered in the anticipation of having his hands on her skin. Somehow they ended up back in the bedroom, and Thomas slowly removed her clothes. Suddenly shy, she turned her back to him. His naked chest pressed against her back as his arms went around her, holding her close. "You are beautiful, Gina," he whispered as he kissed her neck. "Just beautiful."

Leaning her head to the side, she closed her eyes as his mouth roved over her. With his hands moving down her arms, his thumbs stroked her nipples, drawing them into hard peaks. Never had she been so aroused. This was so much more than simple chemistry between them. He was the kind of man she'd longed for all her life. She leaned her head back against his shoulder as his large hands cupped her breasts, gently squeezing, testing their weight and feel.

Thomas swallowed hard as he held her. His thumbs worked in lazy circles on her breasts as he kissed her neck and her ear. Part of him wanted to rush, to throw her onto the bed, to show her exactly how she made him feel, how she made him react, how hard she made him. But he knew he couldn't. If he rushed her, he'd ruin this fragile thing between them. This trust that was building. This trust that he very much wanted between them. Something that he'd lacked in his marriage that was so very important right now.

Her skin was as soft as anything he'd ever touched, and he stroked his hands over her abdomen down to the front of her shorts. When she arched her hips back against him and clasped her hands around his neck, he almost gave in to his primitive urges. Struggling for control, he pushed her shorts to the floor. "I want all of you against me, Gina. All of you."

She turned in his arms and pressed the length of her body against his, her nipples burning like hot pebbles against his chest. Every breath he took drew her scent into his mind. Wanting to touch her everywhere, his hands roved over her as he captured her mouth again. "You taste like peanut butter."

She gave a quick giggle, but when he cupped her buttocks in his hands, pulling her tight against him, a gasp that sounded like a sigh escaped her throat. "Thomas," she said, her eyes glassy with need. "I can't believe I can feel this good. You make me feel things I've never felt before." Was it right? Was it wrong? She didn't want to know right now. She just wanted to feel. Everything.

The rumpled covers of the bed were cool against her back as Thomas laid her down. The weight of him was luxurious, pressing her into the softness of the bed. He released her mouth and searched out her breasts, licking and suckling both nipples.

Waves of desire and need washed over her as he pulled a nipple into his mouth. Her hands ranged over his shoulders and her breath came now in urgent gasps. She didn't seem to be able to communicate what she needed, but somehow he knew and touched her everywhere she needed to be touched. "Do you have a condom?"

"Yes," he whispered in her ear. His hands claimed every inch of her skin. He wanted her, but he wanted to please her more. Before he got too carried away, he reached into the bedside stand and retrieved a pack, fumbled it open and slid the condom on. With his knees, he parted hers and lay cradled between them. He could feel her heat and moisture against him. She pressed her lips together and tried to hide the moan in her throat. But he wanted it. "Tell me. Let me hear you," he whispered, and let his hand drift downward to her center.

The instant he touched her, she gasped, wonder in every sound she made. Driven by his desire for her, he moved, pressing himself to her soft center. "Gina. Tell me what you want."

Without a word she dug her fingers into his buttocks, urging him upward, urging him on. He needed no further encouragement. Opening his mouth over hers, he teased her tongue with his as he pressed inside her hot, moist folds.

With a gasp, she stiffened, her fingernails digging into his skin, and he stilled. "Did I hurt you?"

Gina took a few breaths and adjusted her position, moving her long legs around his hips and holding him close, pulling him deep inside her. "No. It's just been a very long time for me."

Thomas eased back. "It will be worth the wait."

He filled her. Every hard inch of him filled her. Thoughts were long gone as she gave in to the demands of her body and let him set the pace between them. Tighter and tighter he wound the coil inside her. When he moved one hand between them to touch her, she shattered. Clinging to him, she cried out as pulsing waves of pleasure overtook her. Thomas moved with her and hurried the pace. Clutching her hips with his hands, he plunged deep inside her with a groan. She could feel the pulse of him as he shared her release. Gasping for air, she held on to Thomas as he drew out their pleasure to the last.

Wrapped up in him, Gina finally slept, peacefully and without dreams. Once during the night Thomas nudged her awake with stirring strokes of his hands and soft kisses. This was one night that she would never forget.

## CHAPTER SIX

GINA sat by her mother's bedside for three days before the decision was made to take Martha to surgery to repair her hip. There were no guarantees offered by the surgeon or the psychiatrist. The anesthesiologist voiced grave concerns about how the sedation could affect Martha, given her past medical history and current mental condition. Gina understood the risks. But she had to do what she could to keep Martha comfortable and ensure her greatest quality of life. This surgery might work, it might not work, but she had to try. That's all she could offer her mother. There was nothing else left.

Going to the fund-raiser seemed so trivial in the light of what had happened to her mother, but she had promised Thomas that she would go. So to take her mind off her mother, she decided to torture herself at a vintage clothing boutique to find a dress. There was nothing she could do while her mother was in surgery and Recovery, so she may as well make some use of her time. After checking her cell phone to make sure it was fully charged, she headed across the street.

A dress. A dress. All she needed was a dress, she thought as she pushed one after another aside on the rack. And shoes. And hose. And jewelry. And a purse to complete the outfit. But first a dress.

She sighed. This was going to take longer than she'd expected, and she glanced at her watch for the hundredth time in an hour. She pulled out her cell phone to make sure she hadn't missed any calls from the hospital, but there was nothing.

"May I help you?" the clerk at the vintage clothing store asked.

The woman was in her fifties, dressed in good taste, not gaudy, not trendy or old lady-ish, and Gina started to relax. She could deal with this.

"I need a dress." What could be more simple than that?

"So I gathered. Nothing appeals to you, though?"

"Not a thing." Shopping just wasn't her deal.

"OK, well, first of all, what's the dress for?" the clerk asked.

"Dinner at the Boar's Head Inn. Fund-raiser for the university cancer center." She still couldn't believe she was going to go through with this, but a promise was a promise. Maybe she could contract malaria by then. Typhoid was in season, wasn't it? Or was that the plague?

"Oh, lovely! But you're in the wrong section, honey. Come on over here," she said, and motioned for Gina to follow her. "The classics are over here. You're in the more trendy stuff, which won't work for that sort of night out. And you'll definitely want black for this. How are your legs?"

"My legs?" Gina blinked at her, confused. "I've just got the two."

"Well, do you want to show them off or hide 'em?"

Was she serious? "Uh, neither." What did that matter?

"Tea length, then. Shows some leg, but leaves the rest to the imagination. Whets the appetite of every man in the room."

"Look, I don't want to whet anyone's anything. I just want to live through this night without humiliating my-self." Was that asking for too much? Thoughts of being in Thomas's arms again crept into her mind, and she resisted the urge to replay them in her mind. Sitting by her mother's bedside hadn't given her much opportunity to see him. But he'd checked in on her every day and for that she would be eternally thankful.

The clerk pushed several dresses aside. "Aha! This will be perfect." She pulled a black lace dress from the rack, held it up against Gina and considered it. "With your hair and figure, this will be a knockout. I'll have to trust you on the legs, though. Want to try it on?"

"Sure. What about shoes? I need everything to go

with it." Gina shook her head in disgust as she took the dress from the clerk. "I know I'm gonna spend a fortune for just one night." Holding the dress by the hanger, she followed the clerk to the shoe section.

"Everyone needs a classic black dress in their closet. Never know when you're going to need one." The clerk fussed over her for another hour until Gina had the perfect ensemble for the following night's event.

After a long day at the hospital seeing to her mother, Gina fidgeted with her dress. Sequins and beads subtly woven throughout the fabric caught the light no matter which way she turned. Some secret feminine part of her that she hadn't allowed out in a very long time was thrilled with the way she looked and felt. The heat of a blush scorched her as she thought of Thomas and wondered how he would react when he saw her. So far he'd only seen her in scrubs, or shorts and a T-shirt. The clerk had been right—the dress was a classic, and one she could wear just about anywhere. She just hoped she didn't need it for a long time after this. Going to country club events just wasn't her style and made her very nervous. Thomas was certainly more accustomed to such outings than she was. He'd probably been to hundreds of these events.

This was supposed to be fun, for a good cause, so she definitely needed to put her own issues aside for one night, as Thomas had suggested. The nerves she had were just about wanting things to work out right, right? Not wanting to look good for Thomas, not wanting to see the desire sparkle in his eyes again. The doorbell rang, and her mouth went dry.

"Coming!" She hurried through the cottage to the door, battling the nerves that persisted, despite the talking-to she had given herself. Stopping a few feet from the door, she gave her hair one last fluff. As she reached for the knob, she sucked in a deep breath and opened the door.

"You look magnificent," Thomas said, and the admiration in his eyes showed he spoke the truth. He took her hand, gave her a little twirl that coaxed a giggle of delight out of her, and she started to relax. This was going to be a wonderful evening. Suddenly, with Thomas looking at her the way he was, she thought that nothing could go wrong.

"Ready?" she asked.

Thomas held out his arm to her. "I polished my car just for you." He gave a sidelong smile that made her heart shiver.

"Did anyone ever tell you how manipulative you are?" she asked, and placed her arm in his.

While driving to the event, Gina twisted her hands in her lap, fiddled with the strap of her purse and crossed and recrossed her legs several times.

"What are you so fidgety about? Rhonda and most of the crew you know will be there." Thomas cast a quick glance her way.

"It's not that," Gina said, and twisted the purse strap in her hands.

"If it's your mother, I checked on her myself an hour ago, and she was doing fine."

"I know. Thanks again for checking on her. But…I have a small confession to make before we get there." She didn't want to ruin the evening before they even arrived, but he deserved to know the truth from her. Even if it was painful for her to admit. "This won't be my first time at the Boar's Head Inn." She hadn't lied to him, but she hadn't told him the entire truth.

"So you do know your left fork from your right spoon." Thomas slid her a quick amused glance, seemingly un-affected by the information. "You've eaten there before?"

"Yes, but that's not all." Should she just blurt it out? How would he react? Should she just throw herself under the car and be done with it?

"So…what? You may as well just tell me and then we can get on to having fun."

"I was a waitress there. I worked there for several years to support myself while going to nursing school." Shame made her drop her gaze to her lap. She waited for squealing tires and to be ejected from the car.

"So? Lots of people work their way through college

as waitresses. What's the big deal?" Thomas tossed her a frown, then turned his attention back to the road.

"You don't understand because you didn't grow up here. You're taking the hired help to dinner. I was a servant to your peers and your family, Thomas. Doesn't that bother you?" This could be the end of what had started out to be a lovely evening. Some things people couldn't overcome.

"Gina," he began, "I don't care. That stuff doesn't matter to me. It never has, and it never will." He kissed her hand. "You need to live in the here and now, not the past and not the future. It hasn't been written yet."

"How can you say that? You've never lived without money." Now she'd just insulted her date. Great. Would lightning strike her now? She looked at the sky for dark clouds, but saw nothing except a beautiful summer sunset.

"Money isn't the issue here," he said, and pulled into the long circular drive of the inn that was bordered on either side by enormous oak trees. "The issue is that you're feeling threatened by your past and this is the perfect place to get rid of it."

"I don't think that's the issue at all," she said, and felt herself color. How could he pretend to know anything about her life, let alone ask her to give up her past, just like that?

"Gina, I know a little something about this. At some point in your life you're going to have to choose what's more important to you—your past or your future." He opened the car door and got out, then came round to her side.

"That's easy for you to say." She put her hand in his and allowed him to ease her from the seat.

"Sure it is. It's always easier to pick apart someone else's life than it is your own." He didn't relinquish her hand as they stood there. "I can tell you what is probably the right thing for you to do, but you're the one who has to do it."

Gina stared at him. Damn him. How could he possibly be so righteous about this? He had no idea what had gone on in this place. She gave a tight smile, refusing to be drawn further into this conversation. "Shall we go in?"

"Yes. I'm famished." They took a few steps, then Thomas stopped. "I'm sorry if I offended you. That wasn't my intention, and I certainly don't want us to have a bad time. Let's take a little time away from reality, just relax and enjoy. I know I need it. I think you probably do, too."

She sighed and tried to let go of some of the stiffness that had invaded her limbs. "You're right." Tonight she was going to relax, enjoy herself, have a glass of wine and dance herself silly. "I'll try my best."

"That's all I want."

Gina looked up at the gloriously illuminated historic

inn with its forbidding reflection on the lake. From the early days of being just an inn, it had been restored by the university and turned into a world-class resort, complete with conference center and golf course. It wasn't somewhere she'd ever thought she'd enter again after being away for so many years. Not after the scene of her ultimate humiliation.

"This place haunts you, doesn't it?" Thomas asked, and kissed her knuckles as they approached the door.

"It does. I'm afraid I'm going to turn back into who I was when I worked here, and I don't want that to happen." She took a deep breath and put on a smile. "This is where that guy I was telling you about dumped me."

"I'm sorry you have bad memories of this place. Maybe we can make a few new ones for you."

"I'd like that."

Once inside Gina looked around, wide-eyed. So many changes had taken place since she'd worked here. Hopefully the staff had changed too and no one would recognize her. Spending tonight in anonymity would be a huge relief. She didn't want her dampened mood to affect anyone else's evening.

"OK so far?" Thomas asked.

"Yep." She tried to hang on to that sentiment as tightly as she was hanging on to Thomas's hand.

"What kind of wine would you like? Or would you like something else?"

"Just a Zinfandel, I think. They used to have a lovely Beringer."

"Sounds great." Thomas led them to the bar and paid for their drinks. He handed her one and clinked the rim of his against it. "Here's to a nice evening."

"Agreed," she said, and sipped from her glass. "This place isn't going to get the better of me."

"Good girl," he said. With her hand once again in his, he led the way across the room, and Gina had never felt more proud to be on the arm of any man as she was tonight.

After finding seats with the Joneses and several of the staff, they chatted and sampled food from the buffet. Although Thomas didn't engage in much of the animated conversation around him, he observed and laughed more than she'd seen him do at work. This was a good evening for him, too, and Gina wanted to do nothing that would interfere with that.

The chat naturally turned to work and stories were told and retold of cases that had come through the ER. As Gina watched the interaction between these coworkers, who were more like friends and family, she realized she'd been missing this in her life. All her friends on assignments were temporary, lasting only as long as the assignment lasted. These people sitting in front of her, surrounding her with their joy, their camaraderie, their spirit, made her want to hang on to a piece of it for herself. They worked together, but they supported each other through the good and the bad times. Thomas had alluded to that, but she hadn't seen it for herself until now.

"Hey, Gina," Robby, one of the other nurses, said. "Got a dance for me tonight?"

"You got it. I'm not sure if you can keep up with me, though," she said with a grin, and felt herself responding to the atmosphere. God, she'd needed this more than she knew.

"You're on," he said, and gave her a thumbs-up sign.

After the main meal and speeches were over, the music began.

Harold, sitting beside her, gave a long sigh. He clasped hands with his wife who looked into his eyes with absolute adoration. "This is what we've been waiting on all day," he said. "The food was good, as always, but the music is what I want, even if I can't dance tonight."

"I'm glad that you felt well enough to come, Mr Jones," Thomas said.

"Nothing is going to hold me back." He leaned over and kissed his wife's cheek.

Robby approached Gina. "I believe this dance is mine." He looked at Thomas. "If you don't mind."

"No problem," he said.

Gina danced a few numbers with Robby and they

returned to the table. She collapsed into her chair and fanned herself with her napkin. "That was fun," she said, and caught her breath. "I'm so out of shape."

The changing music caught Gina's attention, and she sat straight up. "Oh, that's Strauss, isn't it?" she asked.

Harold listened for a moment. "Yes. 'The Blue Danube.' You're right," Harold replied, and seemed to lose himself in the music.

Gina stood and held out her hand to Thomas. "Come on, Doc. How's your waltz?" After the exhilarating fast dancing of earlier, she needed to slow down.

"Rusty, but I'll take the chance if you will." Thomas let her pull him to his feet.

Leading the way back to the dance floor, Gina tried not to feel anything. Tried not to want this any more than she'd wanted anything else in her life. She was having a wonderful time, much better than she'd thought possible.

Thomas followed Gina, admiring the curves of her hips and the way the black dress clung to them. He was definitely going to have to see about getting her to extend her contract. The hospital needed a nurse, she needed to be closer to her mother, and he...wanted her here.

In seconds she was in his arms. He stepped into the dance. Despite never having danced together, it was the smoothest waltz he'd ever danced. Gina fit against him perfectly, allowing her body to be moved by him, adjusting to the slightest change in direction. Thomas sighed and relaxed into the music, wishing this waltz would last a few hours. What a dream. No woman had ever intrigued him as much as Gina did. She claimed to be the hired help, but she danced like she was born to it. She'd left her hair in a tangled riot down her back tonight, the lights picking up golden shimmers when she moved. With his hand on her waist, the tips of her hair just brushed his hand. Leaning in, he pressed his cheek to hers, closed his eyes, and let the music take him away.

The ease with which Thomas guided her through the steps amazed Gina. The romance of the night, the music, the waltz all swirled through her brain and her heart cramped, wanting more than she could ever have with him. Tomorrow was back to reality, but for now she closed her eyes and let herself just be.

The music ended, but the orchestra slid right into another number, and without a word so did Thomas and Gina. After that dance they pulled apart. Gina took in a deep breath. "Doc, if that was rusty, I'll eat my shoes."

"You bring out the best part of me, Gina. I don't know why, but you do." He searched her eyes, looking deep inside her.

Surprised, she stared at him, unable to move. "Let's dance again," he said, and pulled her back into his arms. The music had slowed and they clung to each other, hardly moving on the floor. Thoughts and feelings flowed like a low current between them. Gina knew she was falling in love with him, right here, right now. She closed her eyes and tried not to think anymore. She just wanted to feel him against her, savor this moment when nothing and no one interfered in their lives.

They swayed in the middle of the floor as couples flowed around them. Thomas pressed his mouth against her ear. "Gina, being with you makes me feel things I shouldn't."

She could only nod. The words, the warmth of his voice in her ear chased shivers across her skin. And she knew she was falling hard for this man. Someday she would pay, but tonight she wanted to dream.

"Do you want to get out of here?" he asked.

Unable to speak, she nodded.

As they parted and left the dance floor someone called to Thomas.

"Dr Ferguson!" a man called, and made his way through the crowd on a direct path to Thomas.

He sighed, knowing there was no way around this conversation he was about to have. "Damn." He didn't want this right now. Didn't want to take his attention away from Gina, but there was no way out of it.

"What's wrong?" she asked, her eyes filled with luminous desire and sudden anxiety.

"I'm sorry, but I've got to talk to this man. Will you wait at the table for me? And then we'll go."

"Yes." She glanced at the man bearing down on them and made her way back to the table. Gina drank down the rest of her water. Needing to cool herself off in more than one way, she reached for the water pitcher, but it was empty.

"You two dance like Elizabeth and I used to before I got sick. Like you were made to be together," Harold said.

"Believe it or not, we've never danced together before." Gina still couldn't believe how easy it had been. So easy it frightened her. His cologne still clung to her and with each breath she seemed to breathe him into herself. Facing Harold, she tried to focus on something else. "Do you want to dance with me?" she asked.

"Oh, not with this walker," he said, and patted her hand. "But thank you just the same. I'm content just watching you young people with my wife beside me."

Gina leaned forward and smiled into Harold's eyes. "Do you trust me, Harold?"

"Yes, of course. But…" Confused surprise covered his face.

"Then let's go," she said.

"Well, if you say so." He glanced at Elizabeth, then stood and followed Gina with his walker to the dance floor.

"Put your right hand on my left shoulder and hold on to the walker with your left. I'll help move the walker with my left hand, and we are going to dance."

For a few seconds it was awkward, but once they moved in mirror fashion, they danced with the walker supporting Harold.

"Oh, I just can't believe this," he cried, and clutched her with his right hand. "I'm dancing again. Even now, I'm dancing."

Satisfaction with a job well done filled her, and she gave him her biggest smile. This night was as much for him as anyone else who would benefit from the fund-raising. He deserved his last dance.

When the music ended Harold hugged Gina close for a second and then kissed her cheek. "Thank you, Gina. Thank you. I will never forget this."

"You're welcome, Harold. It was my pleasure."

They returned to the table and Harold hugged his wife.

"We're out of water," Gina said, as she looked at the empty pitcher.

"I was going to get a refill, but I couldn't find a server," Rhonda said.

"I know where to get it." She picked up the water pitcher and walked to the bar. Thankfully, none of the staff recognized her. But as she returned to the table, her past caught up with her.

# CHAPTER SEVEN

"WAITRESS?" a woman's voice called to her as she passed a table full of expensively dressed couples. "I need another drink."

Gina's heart hammered in her throat. She unfortunately knew that voice. That voice had contributed to her ultimate humiliation. Her heart thudding, unable to stop herself from looking, she turned. There was something about a riveting moment in time that one couldn't look away from. It was like watching a horrific car accident, except you were watching your own accident.

"I'm sorry, but I don't work here," she said, and turned away.

The woman leaned forward, dark, dark eyes that Gina had never forgotten raking her from head to toe, open disdain on her face. "Don't play coy, Gina. You're waiting on someone, just like always." Dierdre Montgomery, prom queen, thief of boyfriends and humilator of Gina Riddles jiggled the ice cubes in her glass. "Time you waited on me again."

Beside Dierdre, Brad Montgomery turned. He had had his back to Gina, and when he faced her, shock momentarily distorted his face. "My, my, my, this is a surprise. Why, if it isn't Gina Riddles back to her old job again. Waiting tables like she did all those years ago." He slid his arm around his wife's shoulders. "Did you flunk out of nursing school or something?"

"Th-this…" she indicated the pitcher as sweat poured down her back "…is for a gentleman at my table who is t-too frail to get his own," Gina stammered, trying to explain, but her wits and her tongue failed her. The flush she hated flashed onto her face.

In seconds she was back to feeling like she had years ago, like someone's hired servant and not worth a dime. Dammit. She'd worked so hard to leave this town and people like Brad behind. This wasn't happening. She wasn't standing here, being humiliated all over again by the man she had given her virginity to and who had then betrayed her. He'd said he'd loved her, wanted to be with her, but obviously she had been someone to pass the time with and sharpen his sexual skills on. She'd believed him. Every last word she'd believed.

And when he hadn't called, hadn't tried to see her, she'd known something was seriously wrong. Deluding herself with all sorts of lies, believing that something dreadful could have happened to him, she'd called his parents' home in search of answers. A servant had informed her that Brad was at the Boar's Head Inn. She'd driven there in a panic, not wanting to think of the consequences.

And had walked in on his engagement dinner.

The shock had been unlike anything she'd ever experienced. She'd stared at him from the door of the private room, standing beside a servant who had let her in. Watching the elaborate party, the kind she'd only seen on television, had been the end of her innocence.

As she thought back to that night, and to how far she'd come since then, a sense of peaceful calm overcame the raging emotions that had moments ago been making her relive the worst night of her life. "Actually, Brad, I'm a very successful nurse."

"Really? A nurse. Congratulations," he said, but the sarcasm almost dripped from every word leaving his mouth.

Disgusted with herself for engaging in any sort of conversation with him, she turned to leave. And came face to face with Thomas. Damn. She didn't want him to see this. Being humiliated was bad enough, having him witness it was almost more than she could bear right now.

The dangerous look on his face made her stop. She'd

never seen him this closed, this angry, this formidable. His icy gaze challenged Brad.

"Is there a problem here?" he asked. In plain view of everyone at the table, he slid his hand down Gina's back and rested it on her waist. The movement claimed Gina as his and elevated her to a protected status. No one would dare question a Ferguson, especially one as powerful as Thomas. No one moved. No one blinked.

"No problem," Brad said, and tugged on his tie. "Gina and I were just reminiscing about the old days, weren't we, Gina? She was just telling me she's a nurse."

"The old days?" Dierdre asked, brows raised. "You and she had *old days*?" The woman tilted back her head and gave a very loud laugh. "I thought you said it was a fling, it was nothing." The glitter in her eyes meant trouble for Brad.

"It was, darling, it was. Just a fling that was over long ago." He took her hand in his.

"If that's what you've told her all these years, I wouldn't want to ruin your story, Brad." Gina stayed remarkably calm, smiling to herself. Brad was the one who should have taken the brunt of her anger for all these years, not another woman that he had duped. Gina dragged in a ragged breath and let out every ounce of resentment she had ever wasted on this pathetic man. "You're looking a little uncomfortable, Brad."

"I am," he growled through clenched teeth.

"Perhaps I can cool you off now." Before she had time to think, Gina dumped the entire contents of the pitcher into Brad's lap.

His tux dripping with frigid water, he leaped to his feet. The slippery tile was no place to be standing, and he crashed to the floor.

"I think I'm through here, Thomas," Gina said, and led the way back to their table. She didn't dare look at him. She could just imagine the stern disapproval he was going to lay on her. That wasn't the proper way to behave. She'd known it, but she'd been too overcome to stop herself. Biting her lip, she turned to face him, an apology ready. "Thomas…"

What she saw made her pause. Though still stern faced, glittering amusement clearly shone from his eyes.

Thomas led Gina to the table, removed the empty pitcher from her trembling hands and set it on the table.

"I thought you were getting water," Rhonda said.

"I got sidetracked," she said, trying to the contain the bubble of inappropriate laughter that threatened to leap out of her throat.

"Excuse us," Thomas said, and claimed her hand. "There's a dance with our names on it." He led Gina to the dance floor, turned and spun her into his arms.

The quick movement surprised Gina, and she gasped as she collided with him, her entire front pressing against his. The power in him, the ease with which he controlled her movements and the mastery of his touch all conspired to rob her of any brain function. She was a mass of liquid hormones raging out of control. Right now she wished they were anywhere but in this very public place.

Sliding one hand up her back, Thomas tunneled his hand beneath her hair, his other hand pulling her hips closer. His arousal was blatant. "That was brilliant," he whispered in her ear, the vibrations of his voice stirring the fine hairs. His was not the only arousal between them.

Gina relaxed against him, fitting her body against his, and tightened her arm around his shoulders. "I should have restrained myself."

"He deserved every ice cube and more."

Gina pulled back to look at him. "I thought you would have disapproved of my behavior."

"Hardly. He and Dierdre deserve each other."

"You know them?" Gina searched his eyes.

"My ex-wife was friends with them. God knows why, they have nothing in common except for spending money that doesn't belong to them."

Gina relaxed against him, contemplating her actions and his words. The bubble of laughter could no longer be contained, and she giggled.

Thomas felt the tremor rip through her as she tried to contain the sound. A reciprocal laugh filled him, and as she tried to stop the noise with her hand over her mouth, he hugged her to him and joined her mirth.

"Oh, my God. I can't believe I did that!"

Thomas laughed. "As I said, you were brilliant."

With his cheek pressed to her temple, Thomas let everything recede from his mind except for the feel of Gina in his arms. Nothing else mattered. Some of the resentment that had been living inside him for the last year dissolved. Being angry and resentful and too dependent on work to entertain him no longer interested him. He wanted what was in his arms. With his hand cupping the back of her head, he tilted her face toward him. Every movement stirred the exotic spicy fragrance she wore into his mind. This woman in his arms impressed him in ways no one else had. She brought out the best in him, her courage made him want to face his own past and, best of all, she made him laugh. That blend was an exceptional combination and one he was hard pressed to resist.

In fact, he didn't want to resist any of it at all. "Gina, I want to kiss you." Her lips parted as she took in a surprised breath, and the sight of her full mouth aroused him even more. "I want to take you home and undress you, touch every inch of your skin, taste every inch of you and bury myself inside you. I want to feel you quiver in my arms."

She blew out a quick breath and lowered her gaze to

his mouth. "I'm pretty close to quivering right now, Doc." This couldn't be happening to her. He was so fabulous, so hot and she was so…thrilled that he wanted her. Living in this fairy tale could only bring heartache she didn't need, but that didn't stop her from reaching out to him.

Desire smudged the vibrant color of her eyes, and Thomas lowered his mouth to hers. There was no pretense between them. They wanted each other. They moved together, against each other, to the slow, rhythmic music and lost themselves in the taste of the kiss.

After thoroughly exploring her mouth, Thomas raised his head. "I think I'm about ready to go." He cleared his throat. "You?"

"Oh, yeah. Definitely." Gina tried to calm the fluttering of her heart as Thomas led her from the dance floor. "There's a back door over here," she said, and, after grabbing her purse, directed Thomas to an inconspicuous exit. "It opens right into the parking lot."

It did—into a secluded, private place, protected from prying eyes by large oak trees. Thomas spun her around and pressed her against the building, his mouth hot and insistent on hers.

She let go of everything. There was nothing else except Thomas right here, right now. His hands roamed over her body, trying to trace every curve and lush valley. He cupped a breast, his thumb stirring her nipple to a hard peak through the lace, and she moaned into his mouth. Lowering her hand, she reached between them and stroked his arousal, wanting to feel his hard strength inside her again.

"Gina," he gasped, and tore her hand away from him. "Oh, my God. What are we doing?" His breath came hard and fast, his lungs burned from the need to breathe. "If you don't stop, I'm going to take you against this wall right now." He'd never wanted anyone the way he wanted her right now, never been this out of control. Never. This attraction of theirs was fast turning into something that he knew neither of them had expected.

The clung to each other, overwhelmed with need. "I'm sorry," she said. "I feel so out of control when I'm around you. I'm shaking."

"There's nothing to be sorry for." He stroked her hair, pressed a kiss to her temple and tried to calm himself. "But I do think we need to get out of here."

"Good idea."

Thomas stepped away from her, took her hand and led the way to the car. The drive to her cottage was tense, filled with the heavy electricity between them. When he pulled into her driveway he turned to her. Without a word she met him halfway.

Tempting and tantalizing, the taste of Gina was nothing short of heaven. His lips moved over hers, and he touched his tongue to hers, gently, briefly, then with a hunger that came from nowhere. He felt a tremulous breath go through her. White-hot desire flashed through him. Somehow he had to resist taking this any further, and he pulled back from her. Smoky need swirled in her eyes, and her lips, red from his kiss, made him want more.

"Thomas," she said, and her hands rested against his waist. "Will you come in?"

"Absolutely." He shut off the engine just as the cell phone in her purse rang.

"Sorry." She dug it out. "Hello?"

Thomas watched as she gasped and tears clouded her eyes. Something was terribly wrong. "What is it?"

Gina closed the phone with a snap. "My mother's had a stroke. They've taken her to ICU and said I should get there immediately."

"Let's go." Thomas started the car again and raced the few blocks to the hospital. Once inside, they hurried to the ICU.

"She's over here," the nurse on duty said, and she led the way to Martha's bedside. "I'm so sorry, Gina."

Gina took one look at her mother, now on full life support, and the dam of tears she'd held back broke. Any meager hope for a reconciliation was over. Thomas pulled her against his side and held her.

"Who's on duty?" Thomas asked, his voice terse.

"Dr Allison. He's gone back to the ER for another patient. I can call him—" the nurse started.

"No, I'll go down and talk to him there," Thomas said. "Gina, why don't you stay with Martha while I go to the ER?"

Without a word, Gina dropped into the chair beside Martha's bed.

After the initial onslaught of tears had mostly subsided, Gina stroked her mother's hand and listened to the sounds of the ICU that were at once familiar and strangely new to her. The slow, regular blips on the heart monitor reassured her that Martha's heart was responding normally. But the overriding whoosh of the ventilator breaths and sighs only confirmed her worst fears. Martha could not survive this assault on her body. If she had been healthy and of sound mind, she might have been able to survive all of the needed medical care and rehabilitation.

When a shadow fell over Gina, she looked up to see Thomas, grim faced. "You're wearing that face you had on when Mr Jones was in the ER." She returned to looking at the pale, expressionless face of her mother. "I know it's bad, Doc."

"The duty doctor gave me all the test results if you'd like to hear them." Thomas brought a chair beside her and sat down.

Gina leaned in to him, and he placed a comforting arm around her shoulders. "Tell me," she whispered, the pain in her heart greater than it had ever been. Though she knew the prognosis was grave, she needed to hear it out loud.

"It's a brain-stem infarct. A big one." The worst possible scenario for any patient.

That was all she needed to hear. "I'll never be able to make my peace with her now." Gina stared through a veil of tears at her hands clenched in her lap.

"We know that hearing is the last sense to go before death. If you have anything to tell her, go ahead. She may not respond, but I always believe that people hear us." Thomas brushed her hair back over her shoulder.

Gina looked up at Thomas. "Thank you, but there's nothing left to say." Her chin trembled though she tried desperately to control it. The pain in her chest burned, and she took a breath. "When do you think we should take her off life support?" she asked. She knew he couldn't make the decision for her, but she needed to hear his thoughts. He was the only solid thing in her world right now.

"We normally encourage families to wait a day or two, have an EEG and an exam by the neurologist before making the final decision." Thomas took her hand. "Gives the family member a chance to…get used to the idea."

Gina nodded and wiped her nose with a tissue the nurse had brought her. The tissue felt like sandpaper on her skin. "I suppose that's fine, then." Another day or two wouldn't matter. Martha was already brain dead.

"Is there anyone you want me to call?" he asked, his voice gentle. "Did she have any other family?"

"No. There's no one." She'd always been alone, it seemed. Even when she'd lived at home with her parents, there hadn't been anyone. No relatives, few friends.

"Why don't I take you home? It's almost midnight," Thomas said.

"Oh, I'm so sorry! I didn't realize it was so late. Why don't you go home? I'll take a cab later." She didn't want to inconvenience him. Regardless of the nature of their changing relationship, he was still her boss. How was that going to work? She had no idea.

"Nonsense. I'll take you."

Gina bent over her mother and kissed her cheek. "It's OK, Mama. Go be with the angels."

They walked to the nurses' station. Thomas gave the nurse several phone numbers to contact them in case Martha's condition changed during the remainder of the night.

"Thomas, you've been way too good to me, and I've depended on you far too much these last few days." She should be stronger. She shouldn't need anyone. "I'm so grateful. I want you to know that."

He tipped her chin up. "You've asked for nothing that I haven't wanted to give you."

Emotions at the very surface, Gina's eyes overflowed with tears that she was finding harder to control. She was so very tired.

He kissed her forehead. "Let's get you out of here."

Thomas took her to his home for the remainder of the night. He pressed a glass of wine into her hand. She took it, but didn't drink. "Come on, darling, have a sip," he said, and coaxed the glass to her lips.

Gina sipped contents of the glass. "I've never been so high and then so low all in one day."

"You're exhausted, I know. Why don't you change, and I'll put you to bed?" He took the glass from her and set it in the sink. A pair of his sweatpants and a T-shirt lay on the chair for her to use.

"Will you hold me?" She'd never asked him outright before, never been so blatant. "I need you tonight."

"Right now you need sleep more than anything," he said, and tugged on his tie, then removed his jacket and draped it over a chair.

"Right now I need you, Thomas. Nothing else." It was as simple as that.

The need in her eyes almost drove him to his knees. His body reacted, but more than that he wanted to be with her in every way. He'd never had such a strong reaction to a woman as he had to Gina. This wasn't just about rescuing her from a tough situation. This was about much more between them.

"I can't take advantage of you while you're down, Gina. I won't." He held out the clothing. She took it with a sigh, but dropped it back onto the chair. Turning away, she presented her back to him and gathered her hair to the side. "Will you unzip me?"

Without saying a word, Thomas stepped closer and slowly drew the zipper down, down, all the way down, past a black lace bra to her hips where the edge of black lace panties peeked out. He swallowed tightly, trying to control his instant, flaming reaction to the contrast of her creamy skin against the black lace.

"There you go," he said in a choked voice and moved half a step away from her. He shoved his hands into his pockets. If he touched her again, he was not going to be able to stop himself. Not after the incident at the inn. He was still half-aroused as it was.

She turned and shrugged. The dress dropped to the floor.

Thomas gave in to the inevitable. From the start of tonight, as soon as he'd walked through her door, he'd known he'd wanted to take her to bed again. Make love to her all night long. He looked from the plain shirt on the chair to Gina wearing a black lace bra and panties, thigh-high stockings and black heels. No comparison. He swallowed again, no longer certain as she took a hesitant step toward him, her glorious hair a waterfall of curls against her creamy skin.

"I need you to take me away, even if it's only for a little while. Will you do that for me?" She slid her hands up his arms to his shoulders, and he knew he could no longer resist her or the feelings raging between them.

"I will," he whispered against her lips and surrendered. He swung her up in his arms and carried her to his bedroom, releasing her legs to stand her beside him. With her face pressed to his neck, her mouth hot and moist on his skin, he shuddered. "Gina," he whispered, and caught her face between his hands. "Gina." He took her mouth with his and there was no turning back for either of them.

It was in her kiss, it was in his touch. Thomas drew his hands up to her shoulders and slowly drew the bra straps down her arms. Bending her back slightly, he nuzzled his way down her neck, across a delicate collarbone and crested the hill of one breast. One hand released the bra clasp and her lush breasts sprang free. Taking one nipple into his mouth, he teased and suckled it to a hard peak. Removing the black lace, he pressed his face to her other breast. Her breath came in tight gasps. "Thomas. Oh, my…" She shuddered as one hand held her pressed close to him and the other stripped her panties away.

Gina sat on the edge of bed. Now urgent with need, she fumbled with the waistband of his pants and dragged them off him. So much of her life she'd hidden in the shadows, but now, with Thomas, she held nothing back. "I want to please you," she said, and stroked him, learning the texture and the shape of him.

"You already please me," he whispered, but allowed her the freedom to explore his body as she desired.

Leaning forward, she parted her lips and took him inside her mouth. Thomas clutched her shoulders at the first tentative strokes of her tongue on his sensitive skin.

Unable to take her ministrations for long, Thomas pressed her back on the bed. He knelt between her feet and rubbed his face against the delicate skin bared above her hose. With his mouth, he explored above and felt the pulse thrumming in her leg. She was a writhing goddess who sought her pleasure, and he wanted to make sure she got it.

At the first touch, she arched her back and cried out. Slowly, rhythmically, he teased her, tasted her and took her to a higher plane.

Now urgent, she pulled him upward to her face, to her kiss, to take him inside her. Each touch, each scent, each stroke brought them closer to each other, closer to something neither wanted to end. Before he lost complete control he tore open a condom and put it on.

With her legs wrapped around his hips, Thomas eased inside her and sheathed himself fully with a cry of exquisite pleasure.

"Thomas," she whispered, already moving with the uncontrolled rhythm that would carry them forward.

Thomas needed no urging as he pulled back and then surged forward faster than the time before. On his knees, he pressed a thumb to her hidden pearl and stroked.

Seconds later she crashed, her back arched as the climax shook through her, wave after wave of pulsing pleasure. Hands clasping his hips, she pulled him harder, faster, deeper, until he almost seemed to become a part of her. His hoarse cry joined hers as they found the wonder of each other together.

Gina clung to him as he lay on top of her, gasping for breath. This was the most precious feeling she had ever had and she didn't want it to end. "I don't want you to leave. Stay," she whispered, and locked her legs around his hips.

"I'm not leaving," Thomas said, and meant more than just their bodies. Too many nights he'd lain awake thinking of just this. He wasn't going to see it end so quickly. He kissed her again and tasted salty tears on her face. "Are you OK? Did I hurt you?"

"I'm fine. You didn't hurt me." She nodded and hugged her arms around his shoulders. "Being with you like this was so wonderful."

"It was." He continued to press kisses to her luscious mouth.

Much later Gina snuggled in his arms, exhausted

from the events of the last week and the untamed expression of passion they had just shared.

Thomas grabbed the ringing phone by his bed at 7:00 a.m. Gina didn't move until he touched her shoulder and gave her the news.

Martha had died.

A week later Gina was staring at the box of ashes on her kitchen table when the phone rang. She let it ring until it quit. Deciding what to do with the contents of the box was more important than anything else right now, including the phone.

Minutes later the cell phone in her pocket rang. Whoever it was was certainly persistent. She pulled it out and looked at the number. A small thrill ran through her.

"Hello, Thomas. How are you?" she asked.

"I'm fine. I called to check on you. You didn't pick up the other phone, and I got a little concerned."

The sound of his smoky voice in her ear made her quiver just a little, reminding her of their last night together. The vibration reminded her of when his breath had stirred her hair and his voice had whispered in her ear. It had been the most passionate night of her life. She would never forget it, but she didn't know how they were going to return to being just coworkers after that amazing time. Every time she'd look at him, she'd remember how she'd felt in his arms.

"I guess I'm OK. I don't know. Everything is sort of…weird right now. Nothing feels right." She turned the box with one hand and looked at it from another angle. "I picked up my mother's ashes a little while ago. Now I'm not sure what to do with them."

"Do you want to have a service of some sort?" he asked.

"I think I should do something, but there's no family, no friends to speak of." She moved the box toward the middle of the table and placed it beside the napkin holder, but it didn't look like it belonged there either.

"Do what you think is best, but don't make any hasty decisions. It's not an emergency," Thomas said. "Changing the subject," he said, "why don't you let me take you to dinner?"

"Dinner?"

"Yes. Have you eaten?"

She frowned. Had she eaten today? "I don't know, Doc. I can't remember. Food seems unimportant right now."

"I know. Listen. Just stay put, and I'll come and get you. We'll go have a burger or something," he said.

"OK. I could choke down a burger and fries if there's a chocolate milkshake attached to it," she said. The words sounded like something she would say, but lacked her usual vigor.

"You've got it. I'll be there in fifteen minutes."

Gina changed into clean shorts and a T-shirt. After Thomas picked her up they went to a diner near the university. Though the thought of a meal had at first appealed, she found her appetite wasn't quite up to it. "Sorry, Doc." She pushed the meal aside and concentrated on the chocolate milkshake. "Guess it wasn't what I really needed tonight."

Thomas reached out for her hand. "I'm not sure anything would really be helpful right now. Other than not being alone too much." He wanted to help her, reach out to her, but something made him resist being overly helpful. Something had changed between them since they had made love.

The first time had been good. The second time had been phenomenal, and it scared him more than anything else in the world. Maybe they needed some distance. Maybe they needed to rethink what was going on between them. Maybe he didn't know how to have a relationship anymore. His ex-wife had done a number on him, and he wasn't sure he was over it yet, despite the pull of Gina.

"Why don't you tell me what's been going on at work? Any interesting cases?" Gina asked.

Grateful for the change of subject, Thomas laughed. He recounted a story of a university student who had taken part in a hot dog eating contest at his fraternity. "He was so sick, I don't think he'll eat again for a week.

I'm sure he'll never look at a hot dog again," Thomas said, and shook his head.

Gina cringed in disgust. "Oh, that's disgusting. Why do guys do that sort of thing?" She shivered in revulsion. "You don't see women having cookie or cake eating contests or anything like that, do you?"

"It's all ego, Gina. Guys are all about being the best, the biggest, the fastest, the most whatever." Thomas remembered a few poor choices he'd made over the years that had all centered on his ego.

"You don't do any of those things, do you?" she asked.

"I married for ego," he said, surprising himself with the admission.

Gina held his gaze for a moment. "What happened?"

"The chase became more important than anything else. Pursuing Constance, the most beautiful woman I'd ever seen, became this personal challenge. It didn't matter if she was really what I wanted. She was a prize that I thought I should have." Now he could see things clearly. But back then he hadn't seen it that way.

"How long were you married?" she asked.

"Two years. We were married before I realized I didn't know her. And when I got to know her, I realized that I didn't even like her." He barked out a rough laugh. "Didn't even like the woman I had vowed to spend the rest of my life with. How lame is that?" Until he'd admitted it aloud, he hadn't realized how lame it was.

Back then he'd never have chosen to marry someone like Gina. He'd have overlooked her for many reasons. But now? He liked her a lot. Maybe too much. And one of them was probably going to get hurt.

"I'm sorry things didn't work out between you. Having a marriage go bad takes a lot out of you." She picked up a fry and nibbled at it.

"Have you been married? Sounds like you're talking from experience."

"I am, but, looking at my parents, I saw exactly the kind of marriage I don't want to have."

"We parted company, and I haven't seen her since. It's better for both of us this way."

"Do you miss her?" Gina asked, not sure if she really wanted an answer to that.

"Hell, no. We were miserable together, a total mismatch." Thomas shook his head. "The hard part was admitting to myself that I had judged poorly and paying the price was totally my fault." Learning to trust himself again was taking a lot longer than he'd realized. He reached across the table and took her hands in his. Tonight wasn't about him.

Gina huffed out a sigh and her chin trembled. "I should have been with my mother."

He knew exactly what she meant. "Why? So you could watch her die by inches?"

"No." She shook her head in denial, but she wasn't

being truthful. "But I should have done something. I was out partying while my mother was in the hospital having a stroke. I'll never forgive myself."

"You were doing something. You were doing something for someone else who needed it. Harold will remember that dance for ever." He threaded his fingers through hers. "You couldn't have known. And there was nothing you could have done to have changed it."

"You're right." She gave him a watery smile. "You're right." She shrugged. "I just wish things could have been different."

"I know." He gave her a moment to collect herself and the silence between them was more comfortable. "There's something else I need to tell you."

Was he calling off their relationship? Had he tired of her already? Did she have ketchup on her nose? "What is it?"

"I'm leaving town for a few days. I have a conference at Duke University that I just can't get out of." He sighed and ran a hand through his hair.

"Oh, don't worry about me. I'll be fine." Somehow she would be fine.

"I know you will be, but I wanted you to know where I was, so that you didn't worry if I didn't call for a few days."

"I'm glad you told me." The pulse that had seemed to be absent in her chest now came to life.

"You have my cell phone number, so call me if you need anything."

"I will, I promise." She could keep that promise, couldn't she? The time, the space would give her a chance to think about what was going on between them. Think about what she was going to do after this assignment. On her assignments she'd resisted anything except the most casual of dates. But now? She didn't know what she wanted. God, this was such a complicated situation.

"There's something growing between us, Gina. But it's so new and so fragile, and I don't want it to go away."

"I know." She smiled softly.

"I'll call you, I promise."

Gina nodded and stifled a yawn that caught her by surprise.

"Tired?"

"Very."

"I should take you home, then."

"I'd appreciate it," she said, and stood. On impulse, she held out her hand, and he took it. That simple gesture went a long way for her. No demands, no requirements, just a simple reaching out. Maybe life *was* that simple after all, and she was the one who was making things overly complicated.

They left the café and walked in silence to his car.

Thomas unlocked the door, but didn't open it, and she looked up at him.

Sometimes words were an inadequate form of expressing deep feelings. Without a word, Thomas leaned forward and pressed his lips against hers. He didn't push, he didn't press or try to take the gesture any further. Then he kissed her cheek and her ear.

At that moment she knew she loved him.

# CHAPTER EIGHT

APPROACHING the front door of the Joneses' home, Gina hesitated. Did she want to see Harold? Could she not see him since he'd specifically called and asked her to come? Before she could think about it a second longer, she pulled the flowers out from behind her back, tried to smile and rang the doorbell. She needed to quit worrying. If she just heeded Thomas's advice, everything would be OK, right? Her inner voice wasn't listening very well. Her inner voice wanted to take the rest of her and run like crazy. But she didn't.

Elizabeth opened the door and ushered her inside after an exuberant hug.

"How are you, Harold?" Gina asked. She presented the flowers and gave him a kiss on the cheek, then sat at his bedside. The hospital bed was a new addition to the living room, but helped to facilitate his care.

"Good to see you again, my dear," Harold said, and

squeezed her hand. "How have you been getting along since your mother's passing?"

The unexpected question brought tears to her eyes, but she sniffed them back. "As well as can be expected, I guess. I'm just used to being on the other side of things, you know?"

"It's a difficult time for you. But is young Thomas keeping you company?" He still held her hand, his grip weak in hers.

"He's been very helpful, but I shouldn't depend on him as much as I have. We both work full-time and that doesn't leave much time to spare." It was the truth, but not the whole of it.

"Oh, dear," Elizabeth said, and sat on Harold's other side. "You've got to make time for yourself, not just work so much. Time is precious, and something you can never get back if you waste it. You and Thomas are young, in the prime of your lives. There's always time for work later."

"Thomas and I aren't really a couple," Gina said, and looked away. Was it true? Wasn't it? Who knew? They hadn't been on a proper date, but she was closer to him than any man in her life.

"Perhaps not yet," Elizabeth said, and took Harold's hand. "But all the signs are there, you know. You just keep running, and he'll catch you one day." She gave Harold a watery smile.

"I'm not running from him," Gina said, and eyed the two who seemed caught up in a shared memory.

"That's just what I said before I let Harold catch me. Of course, that was a long time ago and life was different then. When we met we only had a few weeks before he went off to war. But we've been together many happy years now." She squeezed Harold's hand, and the look they shared made Gina's heart contract. The love between them was obvious. It showed in every gesture, every look, almost every breath. So very unlike her parents, who had merely tolerated each other for their own unknown reasons. This palpable caring made Gina sad, knowing it would end soon.

"Is your pain under control?" she asked Harold, not knowing what else to say, more comfortable with the nurse-patient relationship and not delving too deeply into her own mind. Her relationship with Thomas was a subject best avoided for the moment.

"Yes. Once in a while I have a twinge, but not for long," Harold said. "The hospice nurse has me set up with enough medication to keep the pain under control. Those people are angels on earth."

The three visited for another hour before Gina said goodbye. She wondered if she'd see Harold again. He was looking more frail and his disease was probably progressing quickly. There was no more point in testing to find out the status of his cancer. It had taken hold of him and wasn't letting go.

Facing her life again loomed on the horizon the next day. She had to go back to work.

Numb was the only word Gina could use to describe herself. Ten days had passed since her mother's death and going back to work had been painful. The ER staff had been unexpectedly wonderful, bringing her food, expressing condolences and allowing her to work partial shifts when things were slow that first week. But most of all they offered her a friendship she hadn't known existed. The generosity of these people humbled her. They were a great bunch, and she would miss them when she left for her next assignment.

For the years she'd worked as a travel nurse she'd only made the most temporary of friends. But here, in the home town she hadn't been able to leave fast enough, somehow, through the common denominator of death, she'd found a small community of friends to whom she could reach out. Her life had changed. Her attitude about life had yet to catch up. The question was, could she accept those changes?

Thomas had returned from his conference. They were working together again. And it was…weird. Were they back to simply being coworkers, were they still lovers, or what? Gina didn't know and just tried to concentrate on work, the one solid thing in her life.

Triage was slow until late in the afternoon. She'd placed three people in exam rooms, checked vital signs, taken the histories. Her mind didn't seem to be able to function properly, and she felt as if she was asking the same questions over and over. Maybe she was. Maybe that's all she could cope with right now.

By the end of the day she had a headache, and her feet and back ached. She needed a tub full of warm water and fragrant bubbles for a long soak. Maybe a glass of wine. Gina looked up as footsteps approaching the desk. It was Thomas, his eyes assessing but guarded somehow. Was he wondering the same things she had been?

"Could I have a moment before you go?" he asked.

"Sure," she said, and followed him to his office. "What's up?" she asked as soon as he closed the door, uncomfortable with the distance between them, but not knowing how to change it.

"I wanted to see how you were doing. You've been scarce since I got back from my conference." He sat behind his desk, looking as official as he had a few weeks ago. Had it really only been a few weeks? It felt like a lifetime to her.

"I really don't have an answer to that," she said, and offered a small smile. "I'm just trying to live in the moment, go day to day, sometimes shift by shift."

"Have you been back to the park exercising?" His observant eyes watched her.

"No," she said, and looked down. "Rollerblading seems pretty dumb right now." Everything seemed dumb right now. Even standing here, having this conversation, seemed somehow out of place.

"You have dark circles under your eyes. I assume you aren't getting enough quality sleep yet."

"No, that's not true. I'm actually sleeping a lot." With sleep came oblivion, and she needed that right now.

"You may be sleeping a lot, but not well. If you're suffering from depression, I can prescribe something for you."

"I appreciate the offer, Doc, but I don't want pills." It wasn't the way to go for her, though she knew all the reasons she should try something. "I'll get through this." Somehow.

"Actually, I was thinking more along the lines of dinner, a movie, a glass of wine and a therapeutic soak in my hot tub."

Gina's eyes widened briefly in surprise, and she gave a quick laugh, the feeling somehow foreign. "Why, Doc. I had no idea your prescriptions ran to such intimacies. Is that standard practice?"

"Only for you, Gina. Only for you." He stood and came around the desk. "I know this isn't the best of times, and you've experienced great personal grief." He took her hands in his and the warmth from his skin infused some heat into hers. "Getting away from here might do you some good. Even if it's just for a day or two."

"I'm OK, Doc. Really. It's just weird, being back at work again. When the ER is slow I sit and think too much." Some of her anxiety eased just talking to him.

"Well, I have a proposition for you." He crouched beside her, his gaze probing hers.

"What?" She frowned, her heart starting to beat erratically again after days of pure numbness. Was it just his presence beside her? Was it the memory of their shared passion? Or was it just an irregular heartbeat for no reason at all? As she looked at him, from the concern in his eyes and the way his mouth moved, she knew it was more. He was too good for her. But that hadn't stopped her from falling for him.

"Will you go away with me for the weekend? We could go to the beach or to the mountains. Your choice." He stroked a finger down her cheek. "No strings. No commitments. Just a few days away. Somewhere quiet where we can take a long walk, hold hands and drink a glass of wine in peace."

"Thomas…" Gina paused, not sure what to say. This was a very different direction for their relationship. A huge leap, in fact. "That's a pretty big proposition and I'm not sure I'm ready for it right now."

"I know. I don't mean to push you, but a change of

scenery would be good for you. Think about it for a few days." Gina had gotten to him, and he didn't want to let her get away.

She nodded. "The mountains have always been—"

The intercom paged overhead. "Code blue, ICU. Code blue, ICU."

"Damn." Thomas started toward the door. "I have to go. I'm the only doc on at the moment." He gave a quick touch to her arm. "We'll talk more later." He dashed out the door.

Gina watched him go, wondering when a man with such dedication, skills and caring was going to get bored with small-town life.

There was no point in waiting for Thomas to return. Codes could sometimes take hours. She gathered her things and left the ER.

Not quite feeling like sitting in the cottage alone, she drove to the grocery store. Mindlessly she took a cart and walked along the aisles, but nothing appealed to her.

Lingering in the ice-cream aisle, she collected several kinds of ice cream and hoped she'd make it home before it melted in the summer heat. As she rounded the corner to go to the checkout, she almost plowed into Mary Lou.

"Sorry," Gina said, without looking up.

"Gina, honey? What's wrong?" Mary Lou asked. "I saw in the paper that your mama died. I'm so sorry for you," she said, and grabbed Gina into a hug and held her.

Tears pricked Gina's eyes.

"I don't know what's wrong with me. I'm so sorry, Mary Lou," Gina said as she pulled back. Wiping her eyes with the heels of her hands, she knew she'd just smeared every bit of mascara across her face.

"Don't you worry, honey. Losing your mama is a big event in your life." Mary Lou nodded, and her eyes got misty. "When my mama died—the cancer took her, you know—I was miserable for a long time." She shrugged. "But then you put the dead in their proper place and life goes on. That's the way life is. Bein' a nurse, I'm sure you know that."

Gina could only nod, wondering how Mary Lou had come into such insight. "You're right. But it's so fresh right now. All I can think of are the things I should have done and how I should have been there more—"

"You stop that kinda talk right now. All you could do was your best, and that's what you did. Thinkin' about what you shoulda, coulda done will make you nuts."

"It has been. All I do is cry or sleep." Gina brushed back a few new tears from her face. She gestured to her cart. "Or eat ice cream."

"Oh, I know. I did too, and that's the way you get through it. But you just let that handsome doctor of yours take care of you."

"He's not really—"

"Oh, don't you deny it, honey. I saw the way he looked at you when you were here the last time. That man is crazy about you. Just crazy." She placed her arm around Gina's shoulders, and they walked together, with Mary Lou pushing Gina's cart ahead of them. "You just let him take care of you. Men have a need to take care of their women, so you just let him, OK? It's hard for us women to let people take care of us, but sometimes we just have to." She pointed to the cart. "But don't overdo the ice cream or you'll have hips like mine," she said with a grin.

Gina couldn't help but think back to their previous conversation about Mary Lou's hips. "I'll watch it. I promise."

"Good. Now, you call me when you're ready to look at weddin' cake designs. I'll even give you a discount since we've known each other for so long." Mary Lou released Gina's shoulders as they approached the check-out line. "Here's my number," she said and handed Gina a business card. "And I want your number, too." She wrote down Gina's cell phone number.

"Now, I'm going to call you in a while, just to check in and see how you're doin'. I know this is hard." She clicked her tongue. "But you'll get through it." She patted Gina's arm, and they strolled toward the doors. "You'll get things straightened out with Thomas, I just know it. I got a good feelin' about him."

"Mary Lou," Gina said. "Thomas and I aren't really—"

"Uh-huh," she said, her eyes narrowed and a sly smile on her face. "That man has love, or at least lust, written all over him, and it's all for you, honey, all for you."

She stared at Mary Lou for a moment, digesting the woman's observations.

"It's true, honey. You take that ice cream and share it with him. You'll see."

Gina took her items home and thought about Mary Lou during the short drive. The woman saw romance in everything. Always had. But this time she was wrong. She had to be.

Through with the code, everything wound up for the night, Thomas headed home with a feeling of dissatisfaction churning in his gut. As he entered his house he realized something was wrong. But he didn't know what. The lights all seemed to be working OK, nothing had been disturbed, everything was in its proper place. The air seemed a bit stale. After fixing a sandwich, Thomas settled in front of the television, but too many news stations ran the same outrageous stories, so he flipped the radio on instead.

Smooth jazz. Just what he needed to unwind with. Half-asleep in minutes on the couch, he leaned his head back and lost himself in the music. The ring tone on his cell phone startled him awake.

"This is Dr Ferguson," he said, rubbing his eyes.

"You sound so official, Doc."

Gina's voice in his ear woke him instantly. "Everything OK?" he asked, pleased that she'd called him.

"Sure. Just wanted to see how the code went."

He could hear the hesitation in her voice, so he tried to be as nonchalant as possible. "Successful. ICU's got a good team. But I think we'll probably have to send the patient out to Richmond tomorrow."

"That'll be good," she said. "They have a good program over there."

They chatted for a few moments about work issues until Gina paused. "Doc, about the weekend thing…"

Damn. He'd pushed her too quickly. "Yes?" He left it at that.

"If the offer's still open, I haven't been to the mountains for a long, long time," she said, her voice soft with yearning.

Grinning, Thomas was glad she couldn't see him. "Offer's still open. Anytime." Relief washed through him. He didn't know whether this was a good thing or a bad thing, but at least it was progress. He wanted to get to know Gina better, have a change to figure out what was going on between them aside from fabulous sex. "What do you think Mary Lou will have to say about it?"

Gina gasped. "Doc! Don't you dare!"

Thomas laughed, wishing he could see the redness flare in her cheeks. He loved that about her.

"Oh, you're a wicked man," she said, but laughter hid behind the words. "I don't know why I put up with you."

"Because you think I'm *cute*," he said, unable to keep the grin from his face. "You told Mary Lou I was cute, didn't you?"

"Ha! Cute only goes so far with me, Doc."

"Gina? I think you're cute, too," he said, and wished that she was there beside him. He'd show her just how cute he thought she was.

For a moment only silence came through the line.

"Gina?" Had his cell connection gone bad? Had she hung up on him?

"I'm here," she whispered.

Thomas heard her voice catch and the raggedness of her breathing in the background. He hoped that he hadn't caused her more distress with his comment. "Are you OK?" He cleared his throat. "I was just teasing."

"I know. It just felt so normal that for a moment I forgot about…everything else," she said, then paused.

"I understand. After my divorce nothing seemed right for a long time. I didn't know where I belonged any-more." Still didn't sometimes, but he was working on it.

"You?" Gina snorted in the phone. "Your family is one of the most prominent in the state of Virginia. How can you not know where you belong?"

"That's my family, not me. My brothers never seemed to have any trouble, but…" He paused. "I think I was adopted."

"Thomas!" Gina laughed into the phone. "You're being silly."

"Yeah, but I got you to laugh." And that was worth it.

"You did," she admitted.

"How about I pick you up tomorrow afternoon, and we go to the mountains for the weekend? I know of a little cabin in the woods that's quiet."

"Sounds great. I'll be ready."

The next afternoon Thomas negotiated the Porsche through the Blue Ridge Mountains, up and down winding stretches of highway bordered on either side by miles and miles of forest. Then the landscape changed, and they broke free of the dense woods. A mountain dropped away on one side to reveal the Shenandoah Valley, once the breadbasket of the south. Acres of lush green farmland supported the local economy in many ways and provided fresh produce available for many months of the year.

"I've been here many times, but it's still an amazing sight." She watched out the window at the ever-changing scenery, and a soft sigh escaped from her.

The awe in her voice touched him. Virginia was his home, too, and he loved it. He needed to get away from work more and enjoy it. "The last time I was up here I crashed my mountain bike and haven't been back since."

"What happened?" She turned toward him, her eyes wide with curiosity.

"I hit a tree."

"Were you hurt? Did you have a helmet on?"

He shifted in his seat, now wishing he hadn't told her anything. "I swerved to miss a squirrel on the trail, hit a rock, which gave me a flat tire, then crashed into the tree."

Gina covered her mouth with her hand, trying not to laugh. But the image of this very large, very important man trying to avoid a tiny squirrel was too much. Her shoulders shook as she tried to suppress her mirth.

"Go ahead, laugh," he said with dry humor. "Everyone else did."

Gina gave in and laughed until her sides hurt. "Was the squirrel OK?"

"Ha! He stood there chattering at me like it was my fault." Thomas grinned. "Next time I'll run him down."

"Thomas!" They argued good-naturedly about the situation and who had the right of way on the trails, speeding bicyclists or squirrels. Thomas negotiated a series of turns onto ever smaller roadways until they were crawling up a dirt road filled with ruts and stones.

"Are you sure we're on the right road?" she asked, not seeing any sort of structure. "This doesn't look like it goes anywhere." She squinted out the window into the dense vegetation.

"I'm sure."

"It looks like we're going to the top of the mountain."

"We are."

She eyed him with suspicion. "Wait a minute. You aren't taking me on some idiotic back-to-nature thing where we have to forage for our own food and build our own shelter, are you?"

"Hardly," he said with a laugh. "We'll be there in a few minutes. You'll see."

Gina settled back into her seat, content to wait. Minutes later they rounded the last turn in the road, and Gina sat forward, her mouth hanging open. "You weren't kidding. It's really the top of the mountain." Dense vegetation lifted to reveal his mountain retreat.

Nestled in a dense grove of ancient pines and oaks, a fifteen-room log cabin perched at the very peak of the mountain. The view was fabulous now, but in fall or winter it would be breathtaking.

"Here we are. How do you like it?" Constance had hated the idea of this place, but he'd refused to part with it. Though it was a recreation home, he was more comfortable here in the mountains than he was in the city sometimes. Like now. Sharing his love for the mountains was important to him. He hoped that Gina liked it.

"Like it?" She gaped at him. "Are you nuts? It's fabulous, Thomas, and I haven't even seen the inside."

"Then let me show it to you." The tightness that had taken hold of his heart for the many months since his divorce started to ease.

Thomas grabbed the bags from the car, and Gina scrambled out of the vehicle. He led the way up the polished wooden stairs and the door swung open.

"Don't tell me you have a staff up here?" she asked.

"Just the caretaker."

"Dr Thomas!" A jovial-looking man, dressed in a plaid flannel shirt, work pants and boots, walked out of the cabin.

"Curt, how are you?" Thomas asked, and shook the man's hand.

"All set for you." He looked at Gina.

"Gina, this is Curt Harris. He keeps the cabin in shape and opens it up for me when I want to get away."

Gina shook his hand, too. "Pleased to meet you."

"Have a good weekend. Weather report is a good one," he said as he descended the stairs.

"I didn't even think about listening to the weather on the way up," Gina said.

Curt patted one knee. "This is my weather report. Hasn't failed me in forty years."

"Good to know. Thanks again," Thomas said, and went inside.

Gina followed him into the most luxurious *cabin* she'd ever seen. It looked like a model home from *Architectural Digest* or *Vacation Homes of the Rich and Outrageously Famous*. And here she was, going to spend the weekend in it.

With Thomas. Also the most magnificent specimen she'd ever had the pleasure of knowing. Her throat suddenly went dry. She jumped when Thomas placed a hand on her shoulder. "Let me show you where everything is, and you can make yourself at home. This time away is for you to rest or do whatever you want."

"Lead the way." After a short tour, the anxiety she had anticipated never surfaced. Thomas made no presumptions about their intimacy and gave her the choice of sharing a room with him or having her own.

"I'm itching to get outside. Want to go for a walk or take a ride? I've got an extra bike that you could use."

"Let me change and let's go for a ride."

Minutes later she found Thomas out front, checking the status of all of the bicycle tires. For a few moments she just stared at him. He was so not what she had expected. He was so much more a man than anyone she'd ever known. Just because he came from a wealthy background, it didn't make him worthy of her scorn. She knew she'd been judgmental when they'd first met, but after getting to know him, she knew she had been wrong. Not all wealthy men were like Brad. Taking a deep breath, she released it on a long sigh, blowing away all the bad memories and hurt she'd harbored over the years. With that simple gesture, she did feel lighter. Life was good.

"Almost ready," he said.

Gina couldn't move. She couldn't open her mouth to speak. Everything in her was frozen.

Thomas stood. "What?"

"Thank you for this."

The smile that eased across his face melted her. "You're welcome."

Minutes later they were racing down the mountain on the bikes.

The days were beautiful, but nights at the top of the mountain held a definite chill. Thomas handed Gina a glass of wine and settled onto the couch beside her in front of the roaring fire he'd built in the stone fireplace. Acoustic Appalachian Mountain music played in the background, not distracting from the pleasure of the fire or the peace of the night.

"I'm not kidding. I think it was the same squirrel. He and his buddies have some sort of network going to try to kill me on my bike."

Gina giggled and sipped her wine. "Aren't you overreacting? You're just upset I witnessed your unmanly crash into the bushes."

Ignoring the "unmanly" part, Thomas shook his

head. "Did you see how he stood there, chattering at us? It was the same squirrel. I know it."

"How long have you had this delusion that small furry mammals are plotting your downfall?" Keeping a straight face was not going to be possible.

"You have no respect—"

"For what? Your delusion?" She rocked back on the couch, laughing, and almost spilled her wine.

"For my *right to have* a delusion," he said, and grinned, then ran a hand over her head. At the feel of her silky hair against his hand, he sobered. "Come here," he whispered, not wanting to let another second go by without kissing her.

Gina leaned against him and raised her face. This ease, this freedom he found with Gina was intoxicating. And he didn't want to let go of it.

Tears sparkled in her eyes. "What's wrong?" he asked, not expecting this reaction from her.

"You scare me." Her soft mouth trembled as she said the words.

"What?"

"You…me…this…scares me more than anything." She blinked and a trail of tears raced down her face.

"Is it the money thing?" He didn't want anything to come between them, but he had to be realistic. Money had been an issue with his ex-wife, too, but in an entirely different way.

"It's so much more than money. It's class, it style, it's expectations." She huffed out a breath and took in another. "That's the biggest part. The expectations of…being with someone like you. Of being with you." God, she was such an idiot. How in the world had she ever thought, even for a second, that she could fit into his life?

"My expectation is that you'll be yourself, enjoy yourself and be honest with me." He shrugged, not wanting to think about how her words mirrored his own feelings. "It's that simple for me."

"Nothing is ever that simple, Thomas, you know that. What about your family? Your friends? What will they think about you hanging around with someone like me?" She was so afraid. This was the Brad situation all over again.

He grinned. "They'll be extremely jealous that I have such fine taste in women."

She smacked him on the arm, but his comment had the desired effect and her tears dried. Staring at the fire, she lost herself in the ever-changing flames, the tinge of wood-smoke that drifted into her head, and the peace of being away from work. This was such a magical time, such a fantasy, that she didn't want to move and break the spell.

Thomas curled his arm around her shoulders and brought her close against his side. The snuggling warmth of her against him filled him with an indescribable desire. Not just for sex, but wanting to make her laugh, to be able to dry her tears, to experience so many things together. She was right. This was a frightening situation, and one he didn't want to end.

Thomas leaned toward her. "I want to make love to you by the fire." He whispered more heated words into her ear, and she closed her eyes, taking in his voice, the warmth of his whisper and the passion of the night.

Goose bumps of desire skated across her skin. Not just have sex, but make love. She wanted that, needed that. Thomas was the only one who could satisfy that need in her. She didn't know what was going to happen after this time away from the real world, and right now she didn't care. They both needed it.

Thomas took her glass from her and set it on the floor. When Gina raised her face this time, there was no holding back the longing in her kiss. She loved him. That thought thrust through her on a trembling breath. She had to trust him. With everything.

Standing, Thomas pulled her to her feet and held her against him for a long moment, savoring the moment, the feel of her in his arms. Desire coursed through him as he cupped her face in his hands and kissed her. Gina fit him in so many ways. She just needed to see it. And he had to convince her of it.

Caught up in the power of his kiss, Gina let go of everything that had held her back, that kept her from being happy, and focused on Thomas. This was their time and nothing was going to stop it.

Thomas tugged at her sweater and removed it. Gina's hands roamed over his shoulders and fisted his shirt in her hands. "I want your skin against me," he said. Minutes later, their clothing shed, they dropped to their knees on the rug. She pressed him down onto his back, eager to explore his body.

Giving her the control she seemed to need tonight, Thomas watched the play of colors the fire created in her hair. Producing a condom from somewhere, she applied it to him, her fingers cool against his heated flesh. She eased him into her silky feminine sheath and gasped as she took him fully inside her.

Thomas memorized every movement, every touch, every sigh, as she used his body for her pleasure. But soon he was past being a casual observer and clutched her hips, urging her onward, harder, faster, until they collapsed in a tangle of sated limbs and languid kisses.

Late Sunday afternoon, after another bike ride with no squirrel sightings, Gina and Thomas returned to town. Gina sighed for the tenth time in an hour. "Are you OK?" he asked.

"I don't know. It's going to be strange, going back to work and the real world after this weekend." She reached over and placed her hand on his thigh. "I have to admit that this has been the most romantic weekend of my life, Thomas." And one she would never forget, no matter what happened between them.

Squeezing her hand, a wave of relief washed over him. "Mine, too. But it doesn't have to end quite yet, does it?"

"We can't stop time, no matter how badly we want to." Her life was proof of that.

"For a little while longer we can. When we get to town we'll go to dinner somewhere quiet and romantic, and see what happens."

An hour later they were seated at a small table at an Italian restaurant. "This town isn't very big, but it's got one of the best selections of restaurants I've ever seen," Thomas said.

"I'm beginning to see this town a little differently than I did growing up here." Gina reached for her glass of water to hide her sudden nerves.

"That's good."

"Do you intend to stay here for ever?" she asked, wondering how the answer would make her feel.

"I doubt it." He gave her a serious stare. "How about you? How long do you intend to stay?"

"You're asking a question that I can't answer right now." She toyed with her napkin, not sure how to feel, what to think or how to answer him. "I'm about halfway through my assignment and this is the point I usually start looking for a new one."

"I sense a 'but' in that statement." He watched her intently, unable to put a name to the roiling emotions that tied him to his chair. He wanted her to stay. But she had to want to, too.

"I'm…finding myself not wanting to leave."

"Gina," he said, and took her hands. "I don't want you to go."

"Doc," she said with a gasp of surprise.

"This weekend has been very special to me. I want you to know that I've never taken a woman to my cabin. You're the only one." Could he take it all the way and admit aloud what he was feeling for her?

"Thomas." Tears brimmed in her eyes. To have him return her feelings was so much more than she could have expected from him. She knew he wasn't using her as Brad had. And she loved him for it.

"Gina, I'm finding that I don't want to let go of you tonight. That I want to keep you close by me, and it's right between us." He kissed her fingers and the inside of one wrist. "I—"

"Thomas?" An elderly man, round about the middle, stood beside Thomas and gave him a hearty clap on the back. "My dear boy, what are you doing here?" he asked, then seemed to notice Gina. "Got one of your lady friends out for a night, I see."

"Hello, Gerald," Thomas said with a sigh, and stood. "How are you doing these days?"

"Fine, fine, fine," the rosy-cheeked man said. He tugged on his chin and looked expectantly at Gina. "Who is this fine-looking young lady?"

"Gerald, this is Gina Riddles, a nurse at the ER. Gina, this is Dr Gerald Truman, the previous medical director of the ER."

"Hello, Doctor. Pleased to meet you," Gina said, and shook hands with the older man. She noticed that Thomas had introduced her as a coworker, not as anything else.

"Gina, my dear. Never had nurses that looked like you when I was there. I'd have scooped you up myself if I were younger. But good to see Thomas is putting his time to good use, not just working himself to death, the way I did." Gerald patted her hand then released it.

Despite the interruption, she couldn't help but be charmed by the man. "Thomas tells me that you set up a wonderful program in the ER and his job wouldn't be so easy if it weren't for your efforts."

Thomas looked at her with glittering eyes and a slight curve to one corner of his mouth.

"Charming woman," Gerald said, and pumped Thomas's hand again. "I must return to my own *charming woman* before she sends out a search party for me."

"Give your wife my regards," Thomas said, as Gerald took his leave.

"Well, why don't you join us? We're having a small get-together back here. You know almost everyone here."

"Thank you, but I think we're going to be keeping our party a private one tonight," Thomas said.

"Oh, right. Don't want to interrupt," Gerald said, and moved off.

After a quiet meal, they lingered over coffee, but declined dessert. "I'm full," Gina said, and patted her full stomach. "Thank you for dinner."

He nodded. "Ready to go?" he asked.

After a brief stop at the ladies' room, Gina looked for Thomas, but found him engaged in conversation with another man.

"I know she's attractive, but really she's not the sort of woman you engage in a long-term relationship with," the man said, and shook his head. "You know that, Thomas."

"Why not?" Thomas asked, and crossed his hands over his chest. "There's absolutely nothing wrong with her. She's bright, capable and would be an excellent hostess. She enjoys people, that's obvious."

Hostess? They had never even discussed that sort of thing, Gina thought as she watched the interaction. Eavesdropping was a bad idea, but she couldn't seem to tear herself away or find an appropriate time to interrupt.

"But her family is less than pristine. You know how it goes with us, Thomas. Family means everything."

"Yes, I know. Fortunately, I don't have to worry about it this time round. Gina's parents are deceased."

Huh? What was going on? Gina stepped forward and

cleared her throat. She didn't want to see him pull away from her, to refuse to acknowledge what they had together because of something she couldn't change, like her family. But she could change herself and her attitude and her ability to trust. She knew she could do those things, and she intended to do them right now. She'd come this far and wasn't going to go back to being the woman she'd been just weeks ago. She straightened her spine and had no intention of running away as she'd done in the past. Loving Thomas had changed her, and she had to prove it to him.

"Thomas?"

"Gina, there you are," Thomas said, and reached for her hand. Something wasn't right here. He was looking at her the way he always did. But there was a frown on the other man's face as he watched them. "I seem to keep running into people I know tonight. This is Terry Baxter, a friend of the family. He was just telling me that he's about to become engaged, but is having some… concerns."

Relief swept over Gina. They hadn't been talking about her. She was such an idiot to think she'd hear anything correctly in an overheard conversation. "Pleased to meet you, Terry. I hope things work out well for you."

"I was just telling Thomas here that I saw the two of you together, and you looked very happy." His brown eyes swept over Gina, but she didn't take offense at his inspection of her.

She looked at Thomas. "I think we are."

"I envy that. I think I've been too caught up in other matters to see what was right in front of my face." He shook her hand. "So thanks for that."

"You're welcome, but I didn't do anything." Baffled, she glanced at Thomas, but his face gave nothing away.

"Anyway, good luck to you both. I have a sudden urge to have a conversation with Pamela that's long overdue." He left them standing in the doorway. "I'll call you when we set a date!"

"Do that, Terry," Thomas said, and watched the man hurry out of the restaurant.

"What was that about?" Gina asked as Thomas opened the door for her.

"As he said, he's been worried about the wrong things in their relationship. Not focused on the important stuff."

Gina glanced down at the gravel in the parking lot and kicked a large rock with her shoe. "I've been guilty of that, too."

Thomas raised her face with a finger beneath her chin. "Not anymore, OK?"

"OK."

"Gina, before anyone else interrupts us, I have something to say to you."

"What is it?" Her breath came unevenly through her parted lips.

"I know we've only been together a short time, but…I've fallen in love with you." He gave a short laugh. "You make me laugh, you make my heart pound, and you bring out the best in me."

"Thomas," she breathed, and launched herself at him. "I love you, too."

"Will you stay here in Hidden Valley with me? Marry me? Have my children and make my life complete, as no one else could?"

"Yes, yes, and yes!" Thomas's words filled her heart and banished the darkness that had kept her heart silent for too long.

"Someday we can move on to a bigger hospital, a bigger town, but right now I want you to stay with me." He cupped his hands around her face. "I know it's a lot to ask of you to stop travel nursing, but if we're going to make this work…"

"I will. I will. There's no doubt. I can't tell you how much you've changed me. How much I love you."

Thomas kissed her thoroughly, then hugged her to him. "Let's go home. I'm calling your recruiter in the morning and canceling your contract."

"You can't do that," she said, and slid an arm around his waist as they walked to his car. "You'll just have to wait until my contract is over, and you then can hire me full-time." She paused. "There's no conflict of interest in that, is there?"

"I'm the medical director, and you're highly qualified for the position. But if there are any questions, we'll just go somewhere new, start fresh."

"Doc? We'll worry about it later. Right now, why don't you take me home?" There was no other place she wanted to be than in his arms.

# *Celebrate 100 years of pure reading pleasure with Mills & Boon®*

To mark our centenary, each month we're publishing a special 100th Birthday Edition. These celebratory editions are packed with extra features and include a FREE bonus story.

Plus, you have the chance to enter a fabulous monthly prize draw. See 100th Birthday Edition books for details.

*Now that's worth celebrating!*

### September 2008

**Crazy about her Spanish Boss by Rebecca Winters**
Includes FREE bonus story
*Rafael's Convenient Proposal*

### November 2008

**The Rancher's Christmas Baby
by Cathy Gillen Thacker**
Includes FREE bonus story *Baby's First Christmas*

### December 2008

**One Magical Christmas by Carol Marinelli**
Includes FREE bonus story *Emergency at Bayside*

Look for Mills & Boon® 100th Birthday Editions at your favourite bookseller or visit
www.millsandboon.co.uk

# 4 FREE

## BOOKS AND A SURPRISE GIFT!

We would like to take this opportunity to thank you for reading this Mills & Boon® book by offering you the chance to take FOUR more specially selected titles from the Medical™ series absolutely FREE! We're also making this offer to introduce you to the benefits of the Mills & Boon® Book Club—

- ★ **FREE home delivery**
- ★ **FREE gifts and competitions**
- ★ **FREE monthly Newsletter**
- ★ **Exclusive Mills & Boon® Book Club offers**
- ★ **Books available before they're in the shops**

Accepting these FREE books and gift places you under no obligation to buy, you may cancel at any time, even after receiving your free shipment. Simply complete your details below and return the entire page to the address below. You don't even need a stamp!

**YES!** Please send me 4 free Medical books and a surprise gift. I understand that unless you hear from me, I will receive 6 superb new titles every month for just £2.99 each, postage and packing free. I am under no obligation to purchase any books and may cancel my subscription at any time. The free books and gift will be mine to keep in any case.

M8ZED

Ms/Mrs/Miss/Mr ....................................Initials ....................................
BLOCK CAPITALS PLEASE

Surname ....................................................................................................

Address ....................................................................................................

................................................................................................................

....................................................Postcode................................................

### Send this whole page to:
### UK: FREEPOST CN81, Croydon, CR9 3WZ